W9-ALK-666

ALSO BY ANDREW VACHSS

The Burke Series

Flood

Strega

Blue Belle

Hard Candy

Blossom

Sacrifice

Down in the Zero

Footsteps of the Hawk

False Allegations

Safe House

Choice of Evil

Dead and Gone

Pain Management

Only Child

Down Here

Mask Market

Terminal

Another Life

Other Novels

Shella

The Getaway Man

Two Trains Running

Short-Story Collections

Born Bad

Everybody Pays

Haiku

Andrew Vachss

Haiku

Pantheon Books · New York

This is a work of fiction. Names, characters, places, and incidents either are the product of the author's imagination or are used fictitiously. Any resemblance to actual persons, living or dead, events, or locales is entirely coincidental.

 Published in the United States by Pantheon Books, a division of Random House, Inc., New York, and in Canada by Random House of Canada Limited, Toronto.

Pantheon Books and colophon are registered trademarks of Random House, Inc.

Book design by Robert C. Olsson

Library of Congress Cataloging-in-Publication Data
Vachss, Andrew H.
Haiku / Andrew Vachss.
p. cm.
ISBN 978-0-307-37849-1
1. Homeless persons—Fiction. 2. Street life—Fiction. I. Title.
PS3572.A33H35 2009
813'.54—dc22 2009005023

www.pantheonbooks.com
Printed in the United States of America
First Edition
2 4 6 8 9 7 5 3 1

for . . .

Anna Politkovskaya

Born: August 30, 1958

Profession: Investigative Journalist.

Assassinated: October 7, 2006

Legacy: The Immortality of Truth.

Haiku

Prologue

Just before dawn. Bitterly corrosive cold has descended, creating a bleak concrete wasteland. The street is deserted except for a man watching the ruins of a recently burned-out pawnshop. The man is as motionless as the dead-eyed lamppost beneath which he stands, a single blotch of shadow in a street of many.

The firefighters have been gone for hours, leaving the ravaged building slathered in yellow plastic WARNING *signs.*

The man is wrapped in layers of discarded carpet roughly stitched together to form a sleeveless coat. His head is covered by a hooded sweatshirt worn over a dark woolen watch cap.

Another ten minutes pass before the man crosses the street, moving with such economy of motion that he seems to have suddenly materialized out of the ashes.

Again, the man becomes a shadow, one among many.

As dawn begins to threaten the darkness, the man makes his way to what was once the edge of the burned-out building. Spotting a cast-iron bathtub, he lifts one end without apparent effort before gently lowering it back to the ground a few feet from its original position.

The man flows to his knees, and thrusts his hands deeply into the newly exposed bed of ashes. A faint gleam attracts his eye—a stainless-steel appliance of some kind. He pushes it aside, quickly covers it with ashes, and continues to dig.

Light from the east is beginning to slice between buildings as the man stands up. His hands disappear under his coat.

As if propelled by the throbbing sunlight at his back, the man starts walking.

By the time he reaches an abandoned pier, the winter sun is blazing in a cloudless sky. The man seems to disappear into the pier itself.

In a capsule far too small to be called a "room," the man shrugs off his outer garments and examines his new acquisition: a hand-crafted notebook fully wrapped in oxblood leather, fastened by a tongue-and-groove of the same material. Its heavy pages are slightly yellowed, confirming its status as a thing of beauty from another time.

The man examines each page, using a long thumbnail to separate those that had been age-welded together. Finding the notebook devoid of writing, the man nods as if acknowledging an inescapable truth.

His hands find a slitlike indentation in the wall of his capsule, from which he deftly removes a small jar of India ink and a stylus created from a honed piece of iron. He extracts a tiny scrap of paper from within his coat. Nodding again, he transcribes from the paper to the notebook. Despite the pitch-darkness, his hand moves with confident strokes.

His task completed, the man tears the scrap into minute fragments. Satisfied, he inserts the notebook into a leather pouch sewn inside his coat. It fits as if created for that very purpose.

Only then does the man lie on his back, pull the coat over him as a blanket, and close his eyes.

Sleep comes instantly.

1

"This is the big one, Ho," the man wearing three raincoats whispered to me, his thin, reedy voice steeled with the absolute certainty possessed only by a true believer. He did not face me directly as he spoke—his eyes were focused somewhere beyond the night's horizon.

Every winter, Michael lines his raincoats with discarded tickets he collects from the floor of a nearby OTB parlor. He armors himself with what they symbolize . . . that all the world gambles, but most do so without skill. This is the only warmth he needs.

Michael sees himself as a master of logic, scornful of "amateurs." His faith is as unshakable as his contempt for those who worship the false idol they call "Luck."

That his logic is founded on faith would never occur to him. And I have never pointed it out. It is not my place to do so. I renounced all such conduct long ago, and I have stayed true to my vow.

"Yes?" I said. All I said.

"It's a mortal lock," he assured me. Michael had once enjoyed high status in the financial services industry. But that was when his mind was in perfect synchronicity with his profession, a profession that requires total control of one's own emotions in order to fully exploit those of others.

Michael had spent his days delicately balancing on a

high-wire stretched across a world he now describes only in fragments: "arb edging," "no-cash margin bluffs," "counter-hedge plays." Always painfully conscious of a void deep within himself, Michael kept demanding that the wire be raised. Over and over again.

After many years, his expertise at perceiving risk wove itself into Michael's very essence. He became a believer in the religion of his own infallibility. Too late, the risk-taking he had come to worship finally threw off its disguise and revealed itself for what it was.

The impact of Michael's downfall was greatly magnified by the height from which he descended.

By then, it no longer mattered. Gambling had invaded Michael's spirit and taken it captive. The parasite was not symbiotic. It took without giving, keeping its host alive only by increasingly rare gifts of good fortune. All that remains of Michael today is his demented worship of what he calls "action."

2

When Michael began his prayer chant that morning, I waited patiently for him to finish. Patience is not a personality trait, as most believe. Patience is a skill—a skill that can be practiced only when undetected.

I knew no further encouragement would be needed for Michael to continue; all he ever requires is acknowledgment that someone is listening. My simple "Yes?" was more than sufficient.

This need for acknowledgment limits his potential audiences significantly. Were it not for our tribe, no one would ever listen to Michael. Not anymore.

Our very existence stands against Michael's greatest fear: that, one day, he will begin speaking to himself. All those of our band see such tortured individuals every day. We know this to be the ultimate loneliness.

Perhaps that is why so many of this city's nomads are accompanied by dogs as they travel their circular journeys. And why they will feed their animals even before themselves.

3

"I was over in the slot on Nine, Ho. I saw the whole thing," he said, lowering his voice and partially covering his mouth with one hand, as if to further protect his secret. The taut skin covering his face seemed to draw tighter with each word he spoke.

Michael is aware of his tendency to become excessively aroused; he knows his speech can become so pressured that it feels like an assault to others. He once told me that is why he refuses to stay in the shelters, even when the world out here turns to ice. That was when I learned of his deepest fear.

"They have this 'Intake' thing you have to go through. And they always try and make me see a shrink, Ho. Like *I'm* crazy when I tell them how I don't want to bed down with a bunch of psychos. I tried it once. And let me tell you, these guys are *way* over the edge. If they're not muttering about how they're going to get even with someone who 'dissed' them, they're talking to themselves. And *answering* themselves, too!"

Had Michael confided this to me many years ago, I might have uttered something profound about how humans can be colder than the elements that surround them. But I am no longer in thrall to my own arrogance. So, when Michael speaks, I listen. And try to learn.

This is a technique I taught myself. The most difficult of all those in which I have attained proficiency.

Today, when others address me, I stay silent, shifting my posture slightly to communicate I am paying attention, neither encouraging nor discouraging their flow of words.

Thus, I learn.

The "slot" to which Michael referred is actually a series of coffin-sized dugouts carved into the wood at the base of Pier Nine. The wood had been allowed to deteriorate through a lack of maintenance. The pier itself has been inactive for many years, visited only by ghost ships.

It took us many months to create our place of safety, as we could work only at night, using whatever implements had come to hand on any given day.

The slot had been my idea, modeled on the "capsule hotels" popular in Japan. They allow no room for heating units, but, once properly insulated, the tight, shielded spaces enable one's body to retain warmth throughout the most bitter of nights.

To sleep under such conditions, calmness is essential. I shared my skills by showing the others how to slow the heartbeat, regulate the breathing, and drop the pulse. They all have learned these techniques, to varying extents.

Such learning requires commitment. But what is of greatest significance—no, the *only* true significance—is that each man's commitment was his own. The others were not following my orders; they were not slavishly imitating. They listened to me on a subject I know well, just as I would defer to each of them in their own areas of expertise.

Listening is how I have learned to see the world as they do. And now, it is a world seen as *we* do.

Rather than lecturing about the dangers of plugging space heaters into bridged connections, or burning kerosene pots as they slept in abandoned buildings, I showed the others how calmness within the slots could keep them warm *and* safe.

They listened as I explained that excitement is like alcohol—it temporarily gives the illusion of warmth, but that is soon replaced by enhanced transmission of cold. Each of them knew others who had failed to survive winter's assault.

They find fundamental truth in their own life experiences. This is what makes my explanations acceptable, not because they are the words of some "master."

People descend into our world by different paths. But among our band, certain commonalities had been experienced before our paths had crossed. To live on the streets of this city is akin to standing in the rain: some are better equipped for this than others . . . but rain falls equally on all.

Each one in our band is an individual, which means each

has his own reason. Ranger is still sufficiently connected to his past life so that he regards the slot as an excellent place to hide from an omnipresent enemy, whereas Michael had simply accepted that I would be culturally correct about this method of creating shelter—after all, I am Japanese.

4

Time passed. People passed around us as if we did not exist.

Although his belief system is powerful, Michael is ever-vigilant against being mocked. Just as no evidence was required to sustain his beliefs, no assurances could overcome his fear of being viewed with scorn. But our band knows of my ability to become still within myself, so there was no danger that Michael would misread my patience as silent commentary.

"Okay," he finally said. His tone communicated that I had succeeded in persuading him I would not scoff at whatever he might say, not that I might actually *believe* it. "What about a white Rolls-Royce, Ho? How many of those do we ever see around there? That *has* to mean something."

I bowed slightly, having long since accepted Michael's faith in omens. I never once indicated how this belief refuted his claim that his own gambling was ruled by logic. In our world, contradictions are not confronted, they are absorbed. The same skills used to disable a stranger whose drunkenness induces him to attack also enables a skilled practitioner to restrain a friend who has consumed too much liquor and prevent him from injuring himself.

But this time, I had simply misread Michael's statement.

He was not relating to this automobile as a guiding sign; it was merely the opening card in the hand he was slowly dealing.

Impressed by this demonstration of Michael's enhanced ability to practice self-control—formerly, he would routinely blurt out long, rambling accounts from which one could barely extract enough information to respond—I moved my head in a gesture of attentive approval.

"This Rolls drives right out onto the pier," Michael recounted, switching quite matter-of-factly to the present tense, as if this would help me visualize his narrative, "and then it stops. Out steps a woman, wearing a white fur coat. It was mink, the real thing; I could tell. And she *heaves* something into the water. Something heavy; I could tell by the splash it made."

"You saw a white Rolls-Royce?" Lamont suddenly spoke for the first time that morning.

Lamont's life has prepared him to never even *approach* the border of confrontation with Michael. His voice was clogged and raspy, as always, but its tone was as neutral as stone. And as flexible.

"You saw a white Rolls-Royce?" Lamont repeated. "Driven by a woman in a white mink coat? Was she by any chance a white woman?"

"Yes . . ." Michael said, immediately sensing Lamont's unvoiced skepticism. "But . . . but Ranger was there, too. He saw the whole thing."

"Confirmed!" Ranger snapped out. "Oh three hundred twenty-one. Local plates. Tango, Victor, seven, Echo, Zulu, eight."

I bowed slightly. Ranger does not possess a watch, but he has demonstrated an uncanny ability to tell time without artificial assistance. In other areas, however, he is less reliable: Ranger sees the same license plate on every vehicle.

"Yeah, I know," Michael answered Lamont's arched eyebrows, "but I *was* there, I *did* see it, and, I'm telling you, it *is* worth money."

"Bunny! Sunny! Honey! Funny!" Target burst out.

We do not ignore Target; he is one of us. But we have learned that any direct response to his verbal explosions throws more wood on a bonfire that, if not fed, will eventually self-extinguish.

"How is it worth . . . dollars?" Lamont asked Michael, careful not to repeat the word that had triggered Target's uncontrollable clanging.

"Okay, a Rolls, that's . . . cash," Michael said, showing he had understood Lamont's warning. "Major-league cash, all by itself. Now you throw in the mink. More of the same, am I right?"

Michael's "Am I right?" had been his "closer," a sure indication that he was now paralleling his former life.

"Plenty of people have . . . dollars," Lamont said, working hard at maintaining a non-challenging tone. "They walk right past us, every day."

"When we're out fishing, sure," Michael retorted. By "fishing," he means begging, but that word is not one we use. "But we only fish midtown. Down here, where we *live,* we never see those kind of people."

"It's them that don't see *us,*" Lamont corrected, his own trip-wires having been brushed.

"She *didn't* see us," Michael shot back.

I gave Lamont a look of empathy. I know it pains him greatly when his gift for nuanced expression cannot penetrate the concreteness of Michael's "logic."

When Lamont is not floridly drunk—he is *always* intoxicated, but that is just his maintenance dose—he is capable of astounding subtlety of language. The first time he told me that he had once been a poet, I had replied that a poet is what a man is, not what he does. That, I believe, was the beginning of the bond between us.

"Had to be a dead drop," Ranger said, nodding his head knowingly. He was wearing the Army field jacket from which he had meticulously removed all identifying insignia. "Once you're deep in-country, you can't have the gooks telling you apart by rank on sight," he had explained. "They don't get the name-rank-and-serial-number routine unless they can read it off your dog tag." I understood this to mean what an American soldier recites when captured—I had heard those same words a lifetime ago.

Some part of Ranger is always in-country. He is able to move between two worlds with such fluidity because he never remains totally in either. His mind has learned to instantaneously convert anything his senses cannot otherwise explain . . . or accept. This is not so much delusional as it is adaptive—a self-taught skill.

Whenever he is hospitalized, Ranger regards himself as a prisoner of war. Because he responds correctly to "time, place, and person" questions as if reciting name, rank, and serial number, he is usually released rather quickly. He considers escape to be a POW's duty, and believes he has achieved his release by duping his captors.

This same capacity allows Ranger to perceive me as Hmong, a Cambodian warrior tribe he holds in the highest esteem. For Ranger, "gook" has no racial connotation; it is a synonym for "enemy."

"*Dead* drop? You mean, like when you dump a body in the river?" Brewster stammered excitedly. He is the youngest of us, and extremely prone to inappropriate arousal, especially whenever he has traded his medication for paperback books. Brewster knows he should not do this, but his need to grow his collection is as overpowering as Michael's gambling.

"No," Ranger said solemnly. He is never surprised by a display of civilian ignorance, and always eager to explain his world to those who have never visited it. "A dead drop is a place where you leave messages, so you can pass intel without an actual meet. The VC used them, too. We always searched for 'em like bears after honeycomb."

If it occurred to anyone present that retrieval of a message from the harbor waters would be extremely difficult—and hardly circumspect—nobody said so aloud.

I was grateful for this. When his tales are met with skepticism, Michael retreats. Ranger does not. The last time an account of his exploits had been laughed at by a stranger we had allowed to share the warmth of our oil-drum fireplace, I had been forced to intervene before Ranger could conclude his demonstration of sentry-removal techniques.

"She was getting rid of something," Michael said, slight fissures beginning to show in the eggshell of his self-control. "Whatever it was, it has to be worth heavy bucks to *somebody,* am I right?"

"It would take a team of Navy SEALs to—"

"No, no, no," Michael interrupted Lamont. "We don't have to actually retrieve whatever she tossed in there. All we have to do is let her know *we* know, see?"

"Blackmail!" Brewster exclaimed, awed at the very thought. Such crimes apparently occur frequently in the books he collects.

"Slackmail! Crackmail! Hackmail! Trackmail!" Target muttered.

His last clang resonated within me. Unless reined in, our clan would splinter, each wandering off into the territory to which he was most accustomed—the territory I have been trying to help each of them decide to leave.

"Why have you told me this?" I asked Michael.

"Come on, Ho," he said. "Who else would I tell? We need you to make this work."

5

In Michael's obsessed and possessed consciousness, there is no room for morality. His mind is capable of highly complex thoughts, but all his thinking is reserved for the computation of odds. He has been waiting for that one bet he cannot lose, that "mortal lock," for many years. With each change of season, his connection to reality more closely resembles a frayed wire.

It was through listening that I knew a "mortal lock" in Michael's language meant an outcome literally outside the possibility of failure. A "mortal lock" is well beyond a mere "sure thing." The word "mortal" carries the weight of the term—the "lock" is a death-grip.

The unenlightened often confuse insanity with stupidity. Many of us down here see things not visible to others. Some of those, like Ranger's recurring license-plate number, are images, not insights. But Michael's recounting of events was no "vision." He and Ranger *had* seen the car. They *had* seen the woman throw something in the water. And Michael knows that his once-legendary ability to "smell money" in any situation has not totally deserted him.

So they all turn to me. For wisdom and guidance. As many once did.

6

My name is not Ho. I entered this world without a name. I had no more need of a name than I had of a title.

It was Ranger who named me. I encountered him within several weeks of beginning my walk. Typically, I would hover about the fringes of one group or another. Not seeking admission, but looking for . . . I did not know what. One night, a man walked up to a group standing around aimlessly, waiting for darkness to blanket the city before seeking places to sleep in safety. I watched as, one by one, each person within the group detached himself.

"How come you aren't pulling out?" the man I later came to know as Ranger asked me.

"I am still trying to understand why the others departed," I replied.

"I'm a fucking psycho," he said, as if by way of explanation.

"Ah."

"You're not scared," he said, moving quite close to me.

"I am not," I acknowledged.

He peered closely at my face for several long moments. "I know you?" he finally asked.

"I do not believe so."

Several more minutes passed in silence.

"I got a good place to hole up," he said. "Plenty of room for you, if you want."

7

We spent the next several days in each other's company, exchanging very few words, sharing whatever we managed to scrounge.

One night, we approached a group together. Some left at once, but several remained, falling into place behind a tall, slender black man. As if following some protocol, Ranger proffered two tins of what is called "canned heat." This is a significant offering, because there are many uses for such.

The black man accepted the tins, extended his right hand, and said, "Lamont."

"Ranger. And this is my partner, Ho Chi Minh."

"Ho, okay?" Lamont asked, extending his hand.

"Hai!" I agreed.

When Ranger and I departed that night, Lamont came with us.

Haiku

8

I understood Ranger had meant to confer respect by the name he had assigned me. Ranger considered Ho Chi Minh to have been a master strategist and a most formidable leader of men. So I did not question the name I had been given, nor did I question how a Hmong tribesman such as he believed me to be might have come by a Vietnamese name.

In our world, a man may acquire a name in many ways. In the generic tribe outsiders call "The Homeless," there are both volunteers and conscripts. But this is not the French Foreign Legion; there is no ceremony where a man is allowed to choose the name by which he shall henceforth be known. Some have names thrust upon them, usually as a reflection of their habitual conduct . . . such as the one now known simply as "Forty." Originally he had been dubbed "Forty Fathoms," in tribute to his ability to plunge to the floor of Dumpsters in his daily search for . . . whatever he seeks.

Forty's name had been shortened over time. Not as a rock is reduced by eons of river-flow, but more as though the rock had been deliberately honed to a knife-edge. Little is wasted in a world where some live on the discards of others. Lengthy names are unwieldy here, especially for those who have never disclosed their own in full.

Thus, over time, I became "Ho."

Lamont knows I am Japanese. He also knows the difference between irony and meanness of spirit. Whenever Ranger is present, Lamont's favorite response to anything I might say is, "*Hai,* Ho!"

9

I live among the dispossessed and disenfranchised. But, unlike others of my tribe, I have not descended as a result of damage done to me. The wounds that drove me to these depths were all self-inflicted.

The year of my birth was 1928. My mother earned her living in the only manner available to her. Whoever planted his seed within her was never known to me, just as I would never be known to him.

As a very small child, I was apprenticed to a temple. I am certain my mother did this because she wished better opportunities for me than she herself could hope to provide. For this, I honor her, always.

Her last words to me were "Do your best, my only son!" I clung to those words, and tried with all my spirit to be true to them. As I grew, I learned their deeper meaning. I was my mother's only son because she would never have another.

My mother did not abandon me. Our life was a tiny raft, adrift in a sea of sharks, with few provisions. My mother dove into that deadly water so that I might be rescued. She intended that the temple become my father—a wise, strong, honorable teacher. And, most of all, my protector.

10

I was not yet fourteen years of age when the Emperor's fleet of falcons descended upon America's exposed clump of field mice. Even inside the temple, the vibrations were felt. Our monastic isolation, once highly honored, would no longer be tolerated. With the blessing—in truth, the command—of my teachers, I left the temple to become a soldier.

That command cemented a truth that had been forming in my mind for years—the temple was never the father my mother had so devoutly believed it to be.

But I did not attain the deeper knowledge of the temple's fraudulence until the Vietnam War. I watched as monks incinerated themselves to send their message that the killing must stop, much as the courageous monks stand today against the criminals who starve their own people in Tibet and Burma. The courage of such humble men shames the world.

I remember watching those human torches shining the light of truth. My eyes hazed with tears. I saw then that the temple in which I had been raised had not been worthy of my mother's trust. To spare themselves the fire that lights the Way, the monks of my temple had sacrificed me to those who had abandoned it.

My mother, a lowly prostitute, had surrendered her own life to save that of her child. And the temple had traded that child's life to prolong its own.

Who was more holy?

As that understanding filled my spirit, I knew I had said my last prayer to false gods.

II

The temple was nothing more than a factory, a training ground for those whose life would be spent in service to whoever purchased the product. Because I had not yet learned this truth, I never disclosed to the Army that the prior decade of my life had been a total immersion in the martial arts. By concealing this, I believed I was honoring my mother's sacrifice. I believed I was showing her spirit how deeply I valued her only legacy: humility.

To the authorities, my age was no impediment. There was no need for me to lie. I was *told* that I was seventeen, an orphaned child who had to make his own meager way in the world.

In the military, my physical skills were almost cosmically superior to those of my compatriots, but my worldly wisdom was inferior to an equal degree. Even boys my own age who found themselves in the military were highly knowledgeable about a world I did not know even existed. The world of my mother.

Silence served me well. I wished only to appear obedient, but quickly learned that a blank expression and no apparent desire to speak gave me a certain status. A low status, to be sure, but one that enabled me to learn much more than had I asked questions. Because I was considered dull and stupid, others spoke in front of me as disrespectful teenagers might make rude gestures to a blind man.

I was not dissatisfied with this treatment. The temple had trained me to equate submissiveness with humbleness. But, one foul night, an older man, who was my superior in every way but one, ordered me to accompany him. I acted as if I did not notice the knowing looks exchanged between some of the others as he led me away.

Those looks changed when I returned. I had been gone only a very short time. And I had come back alone.

I slept undisturbed.

In the morning, the others walked around the sergeant's body lying on the field, avoiding contact as if it were a dead rat.

This was before our training was completed. Later, we were all transported into the combat arena.

War alters one's perspective forever. Near the end, no soldier would walk past a dead rat lying on the ground. What once had been regarded as a symbol of odious filth was now a cherished source of desperately needed nutrition.

I merely accepted this, never realizing that I had been granted a foreshadowing of my own future.

12

When the war ended—or, if you prefer, when my country's defeat was finalized—I returned to the temple. To this day, my true motive is unknown to me. I was not returning "home." I had nothing in my heart. Perhaps I had wished to show my teachers what I had learned. I knew only that I must return, and I trusted that knowledge.

But the temple was gone. Not merely damaged—vanished. Vaporized, as if it had never existed.

I made my way back to what was left of the city of my birth. Perhaps I was sleepwalking, dreaming I could somehow find my mother. I was soon cured of that delusion.

Avoiding the occupiers was virtually impossible. Those who found ways to make themselves useful to the conquering forces were tolerated. Some even flourished. But only the darkness of the alleys welcomed those such as me.

It was not long before my skills became known to those who wished to put them to use. The war had taught me much, but the temple had taught me more. So I knew better than to refuse. Instead, I merely vanished. The gods may not have blessed a man who has nothing, but they do allow him to disappear at will.

13

After many false starts, I began to teach. My youth, which would have counted heavily against me with Japanese students, actually proved to be an advantage with the American servicemen I trained. They assumed I was too young to have been a soldier. The tale of my being a child prodigy of the arts, raised in a remote temple that had been destroyed during the last bombing—that was a much more acceptable legend to those who created it. And spread it, widely.

As I taught, so I learned. Two decades passed. Twenty years during which I had no desire other than to perfect my art, and pass this knowledge to my students.

I could not search for the remnants of a temple that had never existed, so I created one of my own. Those who called themselves priests had trained me as one would a Tosa—a large dog to be placed in a raised cage, where it would fight to the death for the entertainment of the high-borns.

I would not call myself by their name, but I did seek purity in all things. I lived very simply. I never tasted sake, I never ate animal flesh, and I never knew a woman as a man would.

I became a monk without a begging bowl. A monk without gods. A monk with ice encasing my heart.

I served only my art.

14

The Southeast Asian wars of the late 1960s brought a large influx of American soldiers to Japan. By then, I had acquired a perhaps exaggerated reputation. I had also developed a working command of English, albeit a somewhat pedantic one.

Immediately following the nuclear-ending war, many opportunities to learn the language of the conqueror had emerged. The privileged classes, the merchants, even the criminal organizations all saw the value of being able to converse in the foreign tongue.

I had educated myself through dictionaries and encyclopedias, studying any "high literature" originally written in English by using its Japanese translation as my Rosetta stone.

The Japanese people of that era reveled in accounts of American racism. Much of our news media highlighted the struggle of those who had been denied full citizenship merely because of the color of their skin. Images of American government brutality were commonplace. The deaths of those who had stood against their oppressors were duly—even smugly—reported, as if Japan were a society in which all were equal.

Hypocrisy became our national pastime, feeding our voracious appetite for evidence of cultural superiority. We were well aware that our country had no need of racism; we allowed only a single race to be "Japanese." Instead of skin color, we separated our citizens by an equally immutable factor—the status of their birth. There will never be an election called to determine the next Emperor of Japan.

So, although my classes were open to all, none were interracial. Eventually, it became universally believed that I taught Japanese students special techniques which I would not share with foreigners. This would seem quite logical to those who spread the myth, since it was accepted that Japanese servility toward our conquerors was a mask. A mask that would be removed in the fullness of time.

In Japan, respect is granted both by and within one's social class. Over the years, I had trained many Yakuza. One day, a man who had been with my school for quite some time requested a private audience. I sat patiently through his lengthy recital of the noble roots of Yakuza, their adherence to a centuries-old code of honor, and how they had successfully resisted all attempts by the high-born to extinguish them.

His recital perfectly paralleled the lies of the temple. In Yakuza legend, great men with deep humanitarian commitment would rescue abandoned children from lives of despair and bring them together to form families whose allegiance to one another was as powerful as the call of blood. Just as the monks we called "master" would address us as "son," the leader of a Yakuza clan is *"oyabun."* This means a father who has chosen his own sons, just as the high priests had chosen us.

In either case, those chosen must consider themselves to have been honored by the choice.

Perhaps this once was truth. A child without a family is an open vessel, eager to accept whatever is offered to fill its emptiness. There have always been such children. Perhaps, long ago, there truly were those who took them as their own, and trained them in their ways. Tradition is created only when practices outlive their practitioners.

But, although I was still a young man, by the time the Yakuza legend was recited to me I was aged in my understandings. I knew the lost children were still sought out, brought into families, and sworn to allegiance. But their "fathers" were no more worthy of the name than were the "priests" who had raised me.

Thus, I waited for what I knew was the actual purpose of his visit. And, as expected, the Yakuza finally conveyed the most humble request of his *oyabun* that I become the exclusive teacher of his family.

Not a word was said about me *joining* the Yakuza clan. It was clearly communicated that I would not be expected to mark my body, or to accept the "tasks" I was to train others to perform.

I was told only that the clan would be honored by my presence. No threat was uttered. But the cost of refusal was as clear as it was unspoken.

For years, several of my American students had been offering to finance the establishment of a school in their country. An investment, they termed it. I had always graciously refused. The evening following the Yakuza's visit, I contacted those students . . . and gratefully accepted their offer.

15

Another two decades passed. I continued to study, to learn, and to teach.

I did not name the style I eventually created. This I considered the ultimate act of humility. My students were expected to follow that same path. Those who insisted on a "name" for the style I had synthesized from a hundred others were quickly culled, as were those who demanded any indicia of "rank." I required all those who sought promotion within the system I had created to submit to testing of my own design, with myself as the sole judge.

I was far from the temple, both spiritually and physically. I rejected the Yakuza as I had the priests. From the moment my childhood died, I had ceased to regard submission as humility.

But, looking only in my own mirror, I could not see the rot that lived within me. This rot was not natural decay, it was a malignant visitor. Worse, it was an invited guest.

A living thing must feed or die.

The demon knew that to reveal itself would mean its death, so it acquired the perfect disguise. Unlike a demon of destruction, such as the one that dwelt within Michael, mine thrived as its host prospered.

Too late, I learned to call my demon by its rightful name: humble arrogance.

16

As master not only of my dojo but of the style I had created, I regarded myself as deeply centered, fully anchored in my new home. But beneath my feet, the tectonic plates of American culture were shifting. My art, once known by very few, became the staple fare of movies and comic books.

Young men would come to my dojo demanding to learn "techniques" that had never existed. Each time I explained that I could not teach a man to fly, or to project his internal force so powerfully that he could injure another without contact, the applicant would nod sagely and depart.

After all, they would console themselves, a true ninja, descended from a long line of samurai, could not be expected to pass along the secrets of the dark arts to outsiders.

This brand of worshipful racism spread like flame in straw. The more I humbly disclaimed, the more was credited to me.

"Worshipful racism" has an oxymoronic ring only to those who have not subjected themselves to the harshest self-scrutiny. One need not look deeply to note that the same Americans who still worship Adolf Hitler are the strongest promoters of the myth that Jews are genetically superior in intelligence.

So it came to be for those of my race. In America, anything "Oriental" was automatically infused with an aura of "powers." Herbalists once marginalized to ghetto existence became the object of chauffeur-driven pilgrimages. True celebrity status required a personal acupuncturist. "Spiritual guides" were a mushrooming fungus.

The "ancient ways" now symbolized some idol to be worshiped. "Asian" and "authentic" became synonyms, as if my race was incapable of producing charlatans.

Young people who could not spell "Confucius" quoted

him copiously. They marked their bodies with ideograms they were told symbolized "Truth" or "Honor." It mattered only that the tattoo artist be a "real" Asian. Even though they could not distinguish a Cambodian from a Korean, the worshipful racists knew that skin color does not lie.

Marijuana-induced mumbling became "Zen."

"Karate" became a unity of mind, body, and soul.

Who could deny such fundamental truths, especially considering their "ancient" source?

17

As our race—the human race—evolved, the love of blood sport has remained constant. What has changed is that such entertainment is no longer restricted to the privileged. Nor is there a need to compel the combatants to participate; today, those who excel are handsomely rewarded.

Because it retains its fundamental root—entertainment—blood sport must be packaged to be successfully marketed. Death is no longer a required outcome. Indeed, great efforts must be expended to *prevent* death if financial success is to be achieved. So such contests now have rules, protective equipment . . . even rest periods.

During the years just before I left my former life, I was often asked to train those who intended to participate in such contests. And each time I attempted to explain that warfare with rules was an antithetical concept, I would be referred to some movie, as if such "proof" would banish all doubt.

Because these children believed in "ninja" as their ancestors had in Jesus, they became easy prey for those who were marginal in skill but masterful at self-promotion. Hucksters preached "Bushido" while selling black belts to six-month acolytes. Movie stars claimed to have fought in underground "death matches" on remote islands. "Grandmasters" told tales of secret missions for shadowy government agencies.

To the unknowing, their own lack of knowledge proves there *are* secrets. After many repetitions, the burden shifts on its axis. An inability to *dis*prove even the most nonsensical claim proves its truth.

I held myself aloof from this. That I did not enter some charlatan's dojo and request "instruction" was an affirmation of my own humility, proof to me that I had reached a level where such trivial matters played no role.

But I never banished that part of myself which noted with pride that *my* dojo had never been so invaded. Or the hidden pleasure I took from the knowledge that none would so dare.

18

Once, I had been respected for my ability and teaching skills. But, as time passed, I came to be revered for my "wisdom." At first—I now acknowledge with a shame too deep to express—this seemed quite justified to me.

Such perception of wisdom ensured that I would fail its ultimate test. I had never acknowledged what I had *not* learned, nor had I ever pursued it.

When I crossed that invisible line I do not know. But, perhaps gradually, my advice and counsel came to be prized not because of what I knew, but because of who I was. Did I fail to notice? Or, more shamefully, did I take such as my due?

In the eyes of my students, I was a . . . celebrity of some sort. And I dwelt within a culture in which celebrities are *expected* to pontificate mindlessly on subjects far beyond their own understanding, with every inane babble breathlessly regurgitated by an adoring press. I thrived in a culture in which actual achievements, even actual knowledge, had no real significance. And, thus, no value.

In reality, it was the demon within me who was thriving, constantly replenished by the harvest of the arrogance I had sown.

The higher the mountain of "fame" I climbed, the greater the distance I put between myself and a state of worthiness.

19

In Japan, students had found their way to me because of my reputation. Many times, I had been forced to prove myself worthy of that reputation. Often, challengers were injured. Once, death resulted. As news of such "testing" magnified with each retelling, the motivation for others to train with me grew. I knew this, and regretted it. But since I myself had never issued a challenge, I believed I had retained my humility.

When I first began teaching, challenges could not be avoided. Typically, they were even announced in advance. I faced each without fear, knowing the outcome was meaningless in the eyes of those who watched solely to judge the character of the combatants.

But in America, I could not defend against what overtook me by stealth. Although my "wisdom" grew, no alarm sounded within me as students gradually concentrated less on my art than on questions such as have confounded the greatest sages for centuries.

My degeneration gathered momentum, to the point where my students would have been disappointed if they had actually understood my answers. They believed that such wisdom as I dispensed would take years of study to comprehend fully.

I had never been trained to deflect such a force. Slowly, my resistance gave way. Or, more likely, I yielded to the siren call of my own egotism.

My speech itself became so larded with epigrams that it left space for little else. "The wind finds its own way" was a particular favorite of my students. Where once I had conversed, I now proclaimed. The humble man who had refused all titles now watched detached as "teacher" or "sensei" turned into "master."

The more I spoke, the less I taught.

The more time I spent dispensing my hollow wisdom, the less I had for teaching the only truth I knew.

20

Within my dojo, a laxness crept in. Training, once focused *on* focus, slid to a level of mere competence. Leaving much of the teaching to the most experienced students, I became a "holistic" practitioner of my art, melding the spiritual with the physical as seamlessly as had the rulers of my childhood.

My rhetoric did not change. I maintained that a true teacher is also a student. By teaching, he also learns. But by then, I was studying to become a master of tautology, spewing meaningless truths as if they were keys to a higher plane of understanding.

For the first time, I began to tell stories of my childhood. Even today, I cringe with humiliation as I recall how some of those stories seemed to embellish themselves.

Self-awareness abandoned me, I would later say. But that statement was both self-pitying and untrue. Self-awareness did not depart of its own accord, any more than my stories embellished themselves. It was I who banished whatever challenged my new persona. I allowed adoring worshipers to gush about how merely being in my presence revealed the power of my *ki.* And each time I did so, I was strangling its very essence.

My mother's legacy of humility and sacrifice slipped away, a beautiful, hand-wrought kite carelessly released, as by a spoiled child whose parents would always buy him another.

We do not value that which we do not earn. My mother's kite of love still hovers, its string dangling. But it has flown so high that I must ascend the mountain of honor before I may reach for it once more.

21

In the world of martial arts, innovators are viewed as inherently suspect; only those who practice the "old ways" are regarded as truly authentic.

When I began teaching, the very concept of female students would have been unthinkable. In America, I maintained this barrier for many years. Such discrimination was looked upon as "traditional." And, thus, elevated in status.

I did not advertise—as in Japan, American students would find their way to me through word of mouth. My investors were soon repaid. That they continued to own a share of my "business" was a blessing. They handled all mundane matters, such as leases, suppliers of services, and payment of taxes, leaving me free to teach. Never did they so much as suggest any alteration in my methods or my standards. This I first took to be earned respect; later, as my entitlement.

I changed nothing. I still refused to award "belts." Students continued to advance solely through the hard-won respect of their peers.

Nor did I permit my students to participate in tournament fighting, because preparation for such contests requires an entirely different concentration from what my style demanded.

Only beginners were permitted to wear the gi. Once a certain degree of kinetic understanding was attained, all further training was in street clothing. Sparring was without regard to size or age. In life, one cannot select one's opponents.

"War" is a word commonly used in America to describe a sporting event. But when attacks are announced in advance, when the combat occurs within an arena, this is not "war." By the time I learned that war between nations was subject to rules—the Geneva Conventions come to mind—I had already seen such rules violated so casually that I had learned the truth of war. The victors make the rules, as they later write the histories.

Other styles concentrated on their rules. In my dojo, we trained to become the victors.

In tribute to the harsh brutality of my own childhood "training" in the temple, I would never accept children in my school. Though I never relaxed that rule, barring females from training was less suited to American culture. Eventually, female students became part of the life of my dojo.

Only in hindsight did I understand—and come to accept—that what I had viewed as incorporation of two cultures under the same umbrella was nothing more than the domination of my own ego. What joined the two cultures was not the study of martial arts; it was the study of *my* teachings.

"Water seeps through spread fingers," I would tell my students, leaving them to interpret what I myself did not understand. When the fingers are opened *intentionally,* the seepage becomes an unimpeded flow. This is why I call my demon by its rightful name: an invited guest.

My "adaptation" coincided with the beginning of what I later recognized as my final descent from purity. For reasons I lacked the insight to understand, the female students were even more eager than the males to sit at my feet and bask in my ever-more-vacuous pronouncements. Such women would train with great dedication, and their expectations were far beyond the attainment of physical proficiency.

What they sought was the spirituality they believed I possessed. But any such spirituality had long since departed.

22

It was Chica who taught me the truth which illuminates the path I now follow. Though she is gone from this earth, her spirit remains, a candle-point in the night, guiding my way. I accept that I am not worthy of this flame of guidance. I know it to have been the final bequest of a child to the self-absorbed "father" who sent her on a mission for which she was not prepared.

Chica was my student, a slender, dark-haired young woman who appeared to be in her early twenties. I knew her only by the name she provided, a holdover from my first teaching principles. In post-war Japan, keeping records would not only have violated tradition, it would have endangered any who studied with me. At my dojo, students signed no contracts; no credit cards or other such methods of payment were accepted. My American investors would create whatever paper the authorities required. This was an arrangement they themselves had suggested, one that I eagerly embraced.

I asked nothing of my students but their commitment. They contributed what they could, it being tacitly understood that this would vary from individual to individual.

That was as it should always be, so that each might find his own path to the Way.

23

Chica was my student for almost five years. She would come nearly every afternoon, often practicing until late in the evening.

Never once did she question the training regimen. Never once did she protest, even when in pain. Her only response to criticism was to work harder. Adversity intensified her efforts. As I gradually descended from teacher to "master," Chica was climbing the path to the ideals I had once embraced with all my spirit.

My art has many aspects, but it attains the apex of its effectiveness only when in synergy with the aggression of an opponent. Those of sufficient knowledge are able to cope with any attacker's apparent advantage in size or strength. But only those at the highest level are able to use such apparent handicaps to enhance their own effectiveness.

In my system, we teach that speed is power. We stress the importance of what we call "being first," but, always, the foundation of our art lies in its ability to convert the energy of an attacker's force into a weapon.

Although we teach avoidance of confrontation, we understand this to be an option that will not always be available. Thus, what others call "self-defense," we teach as attack.

What we do not teach is "analysis" of an opponent. A fully trained practitioner will not "think." Reaction will flow as water against a slightly torn cloth, organically seeking the point of least resistance. Our most complex departure from the hidebound scripture of martial arts is our acceptance of this core truth: Some human beings are of evil mind and poisonous spirit. They cannot be understood, they cannot be changed. And, once they reveal themselves, they cannot be avoided.

When such a person enters—into a room or a life—attack is an inevitability. At the ultimate peak of our art, one learns to *induce* such an attack. When an aggressor moves in response to *your* inducement, he has lost the power of surprise. His assault cannot create that frisson of panic on which he has come to rely. Acting *within* the aggressor's attack creates a narrow slit of momentary confusion. In that moment, the aggressor is completely vulnerable. His power has not been lessened, it has been redirected.

Desire to inflict pain becomes painful.

Desire to kill becomes death.

All speak so glibly of a "center." We do not focus on finding one's own center; we focus on turning an adversary away from his.

Some of the most revered sensei call this "balance disruption." But, just as we do not "name" various techniques, we have no terminology for their total integration.

All styles are rooted in the same basic principle: all attacks reveal weakness, so it is always the aggressor who is at greatest risk.

To attain true calmness within the aggressor's attack is achieved by very few. Many may *appear* calm, but that is most often either self-confidence or stoicism. The true calmness of which I speak is the ability to recognize adversity as opportunity within a fraction of a second. Such calmness is a rare gift—it cannot be learned. But, as with all gifts, it must be nurtured and developed to reach full bloom.

Years of lessons and the most dutiful attention may result in an accomplished painter. But only forces we do not understand produce a Van Gogh.

All such gifts are delivered in two boxes, one inside the other. One is a grant; the other a demand. The larger box may be torn open, as if by an eager child handed a present. The smaller—and far more precious—box is locked. Its key is not provided; it can be located only through devotion, labor, and sacrifice.

To be gifted is inborn. It is not earned. Not all those who are gifted are worthy of their gift. That test lies not within the locked box, but in the search for its key.

24

At some point in our training, pain becomes a factor. This is the barrier at which many students balk, like a horse refusing to jump a fence. Watching Chica approach that stage, I saw that what was a new and even fright-inducing experience for so many students had been a part of her life before she had ever entered the dojo.

It was my gift to see this. As it was my self-absorption that blocked the correct response.

25

One night, Chica was the last to leave the dojo. I watched her sweep the floor. By then I was so entrenched in my own arrogance that it did not occur to me to assist, as would have been proper.

When Chica finished, she approached where I was sitting. She bowed deeply before she said, "May I ask a question, master?"

I returned her bow, then spread my hands to indicate permission. "Yes, my daughter," I intoned.

"Am I ready?" is all she asked.

Did I ask, Ready for *what*? Did I even consider the possible ramifications of her question? Did I give such a dedicated and devoted student the simple respect of inquiry?

No.

Instead, I sonorously proclaimed, "The truth is inside you, child. Allow it to guide you. Follow its path."

Chica bowed, nodding as if I had just answered her Life Question.

As truth revealed, I had pronounced her death sentence.

26

Days later, one of my most trusted students saw Chica's photograph in the newspaper and took it upon himself to bring it to my attention, placing it upon my desk without comment.

The photograph accompanied an account of Chica's death. She was described as twenty-three years of age, pursuing a graduate degree while residing in housing provided by the university. The night after we spoke, a violent confrontation had taken place between her and a man whose name I did not recognize.

The man was identified as Chica's stepfather. He told the police that Tracey—the name underneath her photograph—had surprised him with a midnight visit. However, he had instructed the doorman to allow her admittance, assuming she was going to ask him for financial assistance, as she had done many times before.

But once inside, his stepdaughter had "gone berserk" and suddenly attacked him without provocation. He suffered broken ribs, a spiral fracture of his left arm, and impact injuries to his face.

"I think she must have been high on something," he was quoted as saying. "It was like she was a different girl."

Yes, I remember thinking to myself. *Not Tracey. Chica.*

By the grace of fortune, the stepfather had been just about to put the licensed pistol he carried for self-protection away for the night. He had a special safe for just that purpose, but upon being notified Tracey was already on her way up, he had hurriedly slipped the pistol into the pocket of his robe. Under the force of such a relentless attack, he had no choice. . . .

By the time the police arrived, Chica was dead. A gunshot wound to the chest, at close range.

27

My gift allowed me to watch as the events played on the screen of my mind, as if on an endless loop. I saw Chica's stepfather push a button on his desk, and speak to what I realized must be the sentry at the entrance to his building. I saw him remove a pistol from his desk and slide it into the left side pocket of his lounging robe. I saw him place a bottle of wine and two glasses on a side table. I watched as he opened the door.

Chica entered the apartment, and the man closed the door behind her. She was balanced, aware.

The man seated himself and spoke to Chica. As she answered, he poured two glasses of wine.

Chica approached the large, upholstered chair in which

the man half-reclined. She spoke. What had been a knowing smile slid from his face, as if a mask was dropping.

Chica lashed him with her words. His complexion changed. Anger began to take possession, replacing the confident self-control draining from his spirit.

Chica bent at the knees, so slightly that only a trained practitioner would notice. Venom spewed from her mouth.

Inducing the attack.

When it came, Chica stepped back as if shocked, allowing her stepfather to gain his feet and draw back his hand to slap her face in a gesture so callously confident that it was clearly habituated.

Chica slid behind his outstretched arm, and snapped it with a single, perfectly executed upward thrust. As the man instinctively grasped his right arm with his left, Chica's sidekick connected to his exposed ribs.

The man fell to the carpeted floor, cringing in fear, his throat fully exposed.

But then Chica's training deserted her. Instead of driving her heel into her opponent's larynx, she dropped to one knee and backhanded his face, screaming soundlessly.

Chica was so out of her own control that she never saw the pistol emerge from the man's robe. I prayed that she was already dead as she slumped to the floor, that she never heard whatever words her enemy spat over her before he stumbled to the telephone.

28

Some weeks later, Chica's mother, a Mrs. Lorraine Winters, "spoke out"—the term the media applied to her statements. Again, my student brought the televised appearance to me, this time on his portable computer.

Mrs. Winters told a television reporter that Tracey's biological father was her first husband, a "hardworking man" who had perished after falling off a scaffold on a construction site. The mother had remarried when Tracey was still an infant. "I wanted the best for her," she said. "And I believed Myron could give her all that."

But the mother's judgment had been flawed. When she learned that her new husband had been repeatedly sexually abusing her daughter, she had immediately sued for divorce.

"I made a mistake when I married him," she said dramatically. "I thought it was the price I had to pay to protect my child. But I never dreamed Tracey would have to pay, too."

At that point, she broke into such sobbing that the interview could not continue.

29

A tacit understanding having been reached, my student continued to supply me with whatever information surfaced about Chica.

One reporter was not satisfied with the mother's facile

account. A print journalist who still followed the old ways of his craft, he pursued the truth independently.

That reporter's follow-up story revealed that the mother had not sought a divorce until Chica was fifteen. The original divorce complaint had charged her husband with adultery. The adultery had been his "affair" with the child. That case had been "settled out of court." I needed no legal expertise to follow the beam of the reporter's flashlight.

Chica's mother had never sought criminal prosecution of the man who had abused her daughter. There was some sort of "Family Court" proceeding, the records of which are not available to the public. However, the reporter unearthed Chica's application to attend college, made at age sixteen. That application showed an address different from that of her mother's. Further investigation showed that Chica had been "placed" in foster care.

The reporter also discovered that Chica's mother was still receiving payments from a "structured settlement" she had won in a lawsuit against the company that had employed her first husband. No photo of this man was shown, but his name indicated he was of Hispanic origin.

The divorce settlement with her second husband, the stepfather, entitled her to several thousand dollars per month in "alimony and maintenance." She had also received full possession of a jointly owned apartment.

The stepfather told the reporter that Chica's mother was a notorious fabricator, motivated solely by money. He said he had never known about the structured settlement, and had been told the woman had "family money." This he offered as proof of her duplicity.

The mother declined the reporter's request for an interview.

The divorce documents—which apparently *were* considered a public record—made no mention of custody of the child.

30

Chica's stepfather lived in a luxurious high-rise in one of the city's most exclusive areas. Perhaps this had been a factor in his obtaining a legal permit for the pistol he had used to kill her.

The District Attorney announced that the stepfather's severe injuries, combined with the fact that the attack took place in his own home, made out such a classic case of self-defense that no charges would be filed.

Chica's mother immediately began appearing on more television shows. She said she was writing a book about her experiences, in the hopes that others would learn from the tragedy. A movie was anticipated. She said some of the proceeds would be used to start a foundation dedicated to protecting children.

My student assured me that only a very few would ever read a newspaper investigation, but many, many millions would view a movie. And I had already learned that, in American culture, the movie would become the reality.

31

When I finally accepted the truth of what I had done, I shuttered the dojo, draping only a single black silk ribbon over the door.

My students had expected this. Nor were they surprised at the period of mourning which followed.

My days were filled with self-questioning. My nights were haunted by the answers.

Had Chica truly been the "daughter" I had so facilely called her, she would have come to me for safety and protection, not for meaningless "wisdom."

Had I listened, truly listened . . . I would have answered her question with honesty. Had I known the adversary she intended to face, had I known the battlefield she had chosen, I would have told Chica that she was *not* ready.

Given time, I could have made her ready. That time had not been stolen from me—I had tossed it aside, much as I had cast away my mother's legacy.

Only Chica's spirit was prepared. She had become a true warrior, one who fears nothing but dishonor.

That was the warrior I had taught her to be. The warrior I once was.

Warrior? mockingly echoed within my heart. I was no longer worthy of such a title. I was less than nothing—a sinner who had allowed another to pay for his own sins. I had joined Chica's mother, both of us whores, only for different currencies.

My fatuous, self-absorbed arrogance cost Chica her life.

Worse, it cost her the death of her enemy.

I had robbed the child I called "daughter," just as her mother had. Chica's soul knows my betrayal.

32

For months, sadness suffused me. I remained paralyzed until the moment when I accepted the most bitter truth of all: I was not suffering from grief; I was wallowing in self-pity.

That same night, I walked away. From the dojo, from my living quarters above it, from my life. I did not write a suicide note, because it was not my intent to die. I had not earned such a privilege.

I rejected the code of the warrior as I had that of the priests. A true priest, like a true warrior, fears nothing but dishonor. I feared nothing on this earth, and I was already dishonored. There was no name I knew for a man who has learned to serve something far greater than his meaningless self. But it was that man I swore to become.

33

The priests had taught us that each man has a personal haiku, a haiku that must emerge from within. A master of haiku might be commissioned to produce thousands in his lifetime. But only one could truly express his own spirit.

The priest who told me this later showed me his own haiku. When I attempted to show my respect for his achievement, he gently explained that the haiku was not finished. He would continue to refine it, forever seeking perfection.

"When will it be finished, master?" I asked.

"Perfection cannot be achieved by men," he told me. "Our highest calling is the *pursuit* of perfection. My haiku will be finished when I die, but never will it be perfect."

Haiku

When Chica died—no, when my departure from the Way forfeited her life—I shredded the haiku I had been composing for dozens of years.

Now I have begun another. One of truth. I have rewritten it endlessly since.

It is inadequate. I continue to struggle. Perhaps I will never be able to express what is in me. I cannot know how much time is left for me to do this. I know only that I must atone before I leave, or I shall enter the other plane carrying the haiku of a man without honor.

I understand that renunciation of worldly goods is not true atonement. Many do this, each for his own reasons. Mine is that I must return to the man I was, and so I must focus all my being on that task alone.

I have started my walk. May it become the walk of the warrior I had once imagined myself to be.

I must walk until my haiku reflects the spirit of a man who honors his mother's love, for only then may I call Chica "daughter" when I see her again.

34

I entered my new life with the simple act of sleeping on a park bench. I had been cautioned against this by a group of men huddled around a fire blazing palely in a cut-down oil drum. They had shared this warmth with me in the manner of herd animals, instinctively understanding that only their numbers provide a margin of protection from predators.

As a newcomer, I found my role instantly transformed

from all-knowing "master" to the most ignorant of students. And, as always, there is never a shortage of willing guides.

For most students, a guide is chosen based on the credential of experience. In the world I had abandoned, my students were taught to define this correctly: fifty years of mediocrity is of less value than five of success.

I would use American boxing to illustrate this concept, showing my students that a man may have been a professional fighter for many years, yet not an especially skilled one. He would be called a "journeyman" or a "veteran," but never a "champion."

Thus, there is no correlation between time spent performing the same act and skill in doing so.

"So," I would ask them, "when one seeks a guide, what qualities should one seek?"

"One must look beyond the years," a student might say.

"Look to what, then?"

"To success, master."

"So, then, a champion boxer would be a better *teacher* of boxers than one with many fights who had never become a champion?"

"Yes, master!"

"How does that follow?" I would ask. "Why should it be that a fighter whose physical limitations prevented his success could not later teach others what he had learned but could never himself execute?"

My students would bow their heads. But I never allowed myself to be satisfied with what I knew to be reflexive submission rather than any indication of acquired knowledge.

"There are those who *overcome* a lack of fighting skills due to sheer strength or speed. Such a fighter may often defeat a more highly skilled opponent. But only the *defeated* opponent possesses skills which can be taught to others.

"Do you understand? It was only those skills which allowed the defeated fighter to survive against those who were more naturally gifted. One does not *teach* physical strength; one teaches how to most skillfully *apply* whatever physical strength the student already possesses."

As my students raised their eyes to mine, I would give them a simple illustration.

"Imagine a boxer who had no punching power," I would tell them. "He can *land* his blows easily—swiftly, and with precision—but they have no real effect on his opponent. Imagine another, with very limited skills. He rarely succeeds in landing a blow, but, when he does, it is *instantly* effective. Which would you choose as *your* teacher?"

Then I would see the truth reflected in the eyes of my students. And the subtle difference in how they bowed their heads in response to what they had just been taught.

My sin had been arrogance, not hypocrisy. So I welcomed the opportunity to become a student of those who had been judged failures, mindful that they *lived* in a world in which those who judged them would not survive a single night.

I listened as I taught my students to listen—humbly, but with discernment. I measured any offered knowledge not by how long the guide had managed to survive, but by how he had done so. I decided I would heed only the words of those who had lost all, yet still retained themselves.

53

53

"Don't ever go in those shelters," I had been warned, that first night by the fire. "An old man like you, they'd eat you alive."

"And don't go near the park at night, neither," another said. "Those benches *look* good—keep you off the ground and all—but that's where the kids go to hunt."

"Hunt?" I asked.

"This here's what you call a *bon*fire," the first one told me, pointing at the oil drum. I could see by his manner and bearing that he was accustomed to being the spokesman for his group. "What those evil fucking kids do is what they call making a *bum*fire. And that's us—bums.

"All they need is to catch one of us sleeping. They got these plastic squeeze bottles full of gasoline. Spray you all over, strike a match, and *whoosh*!" he said, pointedly looking down at the blazing fire.

"Could you not protect one another?" I asked. Mine was not a challenging query, it was the speech of a humble man in search of knowledge. "Perhaps by taking turns sleeping, so some could always keep watch?"

"Even if we *could* do that—and who's going to trust their life to one of *us* staying awake?—it wouldn't do no good," the leader told me. "Those kids, they don't just carry spray bottles. They got baseball bats, lead pipes, all kinds of stuff to break bones with. And they *like* doing it, fucking us up for kicks."

I knew he spoke the truth. I had first encountered such men when I had been a soldier. They came in many uniforms.

36

Later that same night, I wrapped myself in a piece of discarded carpet I had found in an alley, lay down on a park bench, and closed my eyes.

They were not long in coming. Even had I actually been asleep, I would have sensed their presence—their collective spirit emitted a thick, putrid odor, like raw sewage.

Through slitted eyes, I saw three young men in identical black outfits, their faces covered with ski masks. Only the red laces on their heavy boots disturbed the total blackness of their images.

As they began their preparations, I slipped out of the carpet into the darkness. Two of them began spraying the thick, empty bundle on the bench, never noticing that their comrade behind them was already immobilized.

37

I left them on the ground, next to the bench. Nothing they might tell the police when they regained consciousness would represent any danger to me. The plastic bottles of gasoline would speak louder than any lie they might concoct, as would the swastika tattoo on the broken neck of the largest one.

This justice brought me no closer to Chica's candle-point flame. Nor did I confuse it with an act of atonement.

But I did tell myself that I had truly begun my journey. In this, I was wrong.

I had sworn to renounce followers, but there are no secrets in a world where there is no place to hide them. My encounter with the would-be torturers was known within minutes, and magnified within hours. Within days, I had become a walking myth. But this obvious parallel to the original growth of my reputation as a teacher never penetrated my arrogance-armored consciousness.

38

"We could find that woman," Michael enthused. "I know we could."

"Surveillance grid," Ranger agreed. "Stage one. Then we set up a box tail until we locate their HQ."

I exchanged looks with Lamont. He nodded sadly. If we allowed Michael and Ranger to pursue the elusive automobile on their own, the consequences were quite predictable. And unacceptable.

"This can be done," I told my brothers. "But only if we do not act rashly."

"You're the boss, Ho," Michael said, instantly.

"I am not the—" I stopped myself from repeating what had come to be my ever-ignored mantra. "Let us go to the pier," I finished, lamely. I never ceased my attempts to persuade the others to stop viewing my proposals as commands, but I had not yet been totally successful. Perhaps not even partially so.

39

Two hours later, Michael walked us through what he had observed. He showed us where the white Rolls-Royce had come to a stop, then began to pace off the short distance to the edge of the pier. I urged caution; the wooden flooring was badly decayed in many spots, and the footing was treacherous.

"Right there," Michael said, pointing.

We all looked down at the oily black water.

"Those big ships used to pull up to offload right where we're standing now," Lamont said. "That means the water's *deep.*"

"It made a hard sound when it hit," Michael said. "Like it was real heavy."

"But small enough to carry in her hand?"

"That's right, Ho. In *one* hand, matter of fact."

"A rod!" Brewster blurted out.

"A what?" Ranger demanded.

"A gat, a heater, a . . . a . . . pistol," Brewster told him.

"A piece?" Ranger snarled. "Why didn't you just fucking say so, man? What kind? Revolver, semi-auto, half—?"

"*I* didn't see it," Brewster reminded him.

"Then why did you *say* it was a—?"

"Brewster was surmising," I said to Ranger, very gently. When I was a child, one of the exercises we practiced was to reach into a nest of tiny candles burning in the darkness and extinguish whichever one our teacher demanded, without disturbing the others.

"An educated guess," Lamont explained, in response to Ranger's quizzical look. "But it didn't have to be a pistol. Could have been anything small and solid. A bundle of computer disks, videocassettes, even a book of pictures . . . Like

Michael said, we're not going to try and actually find whatever it was. We don't *need* to, okay?"

"Define the mission!" Ranger snapped out.

"Well, like we were—"

"Only the commander defines the mission," Ranger warned Lamont, his voice on the razor edge between adamant and dangerous.

Again forced by a more immediate need, I reluctantly temporarily resumed the mantle of leadership I had renounced. "It is too late to begin our search," I said. "But, even as we sleep tonight, we can be alert to the prospect of the car returning . . . perhaps with search equipment. If no one appears, tomorrow we will go about our usual business. Then, when darkness comes, perhaps we could meet in Brewster's library?"

I made the last portion of my statement into a request, bowing when Brewster nodded his acceptance. "Are we agreed, then?" I concluded.

Only Target did not respond, for which we were all duly grateful.

40

I awoke the next morning mindful of the complex task I faced. For some time, it had been necessary that Michael and Ranger be kept apart as much as possible. Ranger was a few years younger than Michael, and often pointed out that while he had been fighting in some foul jungle, Michael had been living in luxury. Michael was not reluctant to defend himself on this issue, insisting that his avoidance of conscription should be attributed to his political convictions.

Lamont seeks what he believes to be the irony inherent in all things, as if to prove that the universe consists of nothing but the random intersection of events. He took it upon himself to resolve the conflict between the two men by establishing their common ground.

Sipping from his brown-bagged bottle of wine, gesturing with his cigarette, seated on a wooden box as the rest of us watched from the ground, Lamont became a university professor, speaking from a position of authority. "Break it down, it always comes back around," he said. "Ranger volunteers; Michael slips past the draft. On different sides of the world, body *and* mind. But that was then. Now you're both standing on one tiny little spot on this planet. And how you got this close is exactly the same way you got so far apart. Only, this time, it was Michael who volunteered and Ranger who got drafted."

"How did I—?"

"You gambled it all away," Lamont cut Michael off. "Nobody made you do it. Maybe you expected it to turn out different, but it was your choice. Ranger, nobody *made* him join the Army. You were seventeen, right?"

"On my birthday," Ranger affirmed.

"Which means you couldn't be drafted. So you made a choice, just like Michael did. And it didn't turn out the way *you* expected, either."

Lamont looked from one man to the other. Seeing no resistance, he went on: "Get it? Michael, you volunteered to be here. With us, I mean. But, Ranger, you didn't ask for any of this, am I right?"

"The fucking VA said I was—"

"The fucking VA *drafted* you, brother. Right into *this* war. Yeah?"

Silence came. Then Ranger nodded, not noticing that Michael was doing the same.

Since that time, an uneasy tolerance had grown between the two men. But I knew each remained combustible in his own way, and feared any attempt they made to work together could be potentially lethal. I subordinated my desire to avoid being anyone's "commander" to the group's need for survival.

41

I was not surprised to find Lamont waiting in the doorway of a waterfront bar he knew I would pass as I ventured forth each morning. That doorway was a safe place to rest—the bar would not open for hours. Lamont held a large paper cup in both hands. I assumed that at least a portion of its contents was coffee.

As a youth, Lamont had been the leader of a warrior tribe. As he related to me one night, "I was an OG before those little 'gangstas' made up the word. That was when gangs *ruled* the streets, Ho. Some streets, anyway. And when you went down on another club, you did it face-up. You *walked* over to them. They *walked* over to you. The newspapers called that a 'rumble,' but we called it what it was—a *meet.*"

As he spoke, I saw Chica in my mind, starting her walk.

"We always duked it out. Fists first. Then chains, blades, nailed broomsticks, sawed-off baseball bats. Sometimes there'd be a zip gun, but that's nothing but a car antenna and a rubber band—you had to be *close* to make it work. Those days, you *earned* face when you *showed* face. Man-to-man.

"Everyone *expected* the leader to be first up, not like some faggot general standing on a hill, watching his men do battle.

"You know how they do it today? Carful of punks drive past a corner, pull their nines, close their eyes, and hose everything down. And they think that chickenshit makes them *men.*"

"It does seem cowardly" was all I could offer my friend.

"I'm not talking about heart, Ho. Ever listen to Ranger when he goes off into one of his war stories? It's like his antenna is all of a sudden picking up a clear signal, no static. But if you look at it straight, you see: no matter what people *say* a war's about, it's really always about the same thing—rep."

"But you explained—"

"Explained? Man, I was just cherry-picking, Ho."

Seeing the expression on my face, Lamont expanded my vocabulary. "I mean, I was telling you about the good parts like they was the *only* parts. You really interested in this ancient gang-fighting stuff?"

"I want to learn."

Lamont studied my face for a long moment. I opened myself to his silent interrogation. Finally, he extended a clenched fist. I imitated his gesture. He tapped my fist with his, as if sealing a bargain. Then he lit another cigarette, and began to guide me through a world that no longer existed.

"Any club was always about *turf.* Like, say, Fifth Street was your block, from Amsterdam to the Park, okay?"

"But that would be—"

"Up in Harlem, when we'd say Fifth, we'd mean a *Hundred* and Fifth," in response to the confusion on my face. "Anyway, it wouldn't matter what little block it was: if you claimed it, you had to *hold* it. Some clubs, they claimed whole pieces of the city. You couldn't walk through their turf unless you paid tolls. Not money," he said, again responding to my confused look, "although, if you *had* any, you could forget about holding on to it. Mostly, you'd just get your ass kicked. But if you flew your colors—like wearing your club jacket—you could get yourself seriously fucked up."

"But none of these clubs could actually own—"

"Amen, brother! You just pulled the covers off. That was it. That was it, in spades. And spics, too," he said, chuckling at his own joke. "We never owned *shit.* But we killed each other to keep calling it ours, anyway."

"If you knew this—?"

"How were we *gonna* know it? Who was gonna tell us? Who was even gonna *talk* to us? Some social worker? You want to know what's really funny, Ho? The City had these guys—college boys, white guys, all of them. They'd put them out in the street for that social-work stuff. 'Detached workers,' they called them. They'd hang with you, try and talk you into going back to school, giving up bopping . . . like fucking missionaries in Africa. But it was doomed from jump. See, the only way a club qualified for one of those workers was behind being feared. It was like a status thing, having one of those workers. Good for your rep."

"So, the more hotly a gang would pursue its . . . rep, the more likely it would be assigned a worker?" I asked. "And if having a worker enhanced the gang's rep . . ."

"Full-circle," Lamont said, smiling.

"But if every little block—?"

"I said claim *and* hold, bro. That's how the huge clubs got all their power. The Chaplains, the Bishops, the Enchanters—what they did was take over a lot of the small clubs. And they did it slick, too. You tell the President of some ten-man club that now he's a flunky, he's *got* to go to war behind that. But if you show him some respect, ask him to 'affiliate,' his rep goes *up,* not down. So his little club, now it's a chapter in a *big* one, you with me?"

"It is a clever tactic."

"Double-slick," Lamont said. "Because the big clubs, they won't even *ask* unless you first show you got the stuff."

"By fighting?"

"That was it. Nothing else would do it. And it had to be face-to-face, like I said. But once you got with one of the big clubs, then it was open season. We still had meets, only now you had clubs Japping each other in their own territories."

If Lamont expected me to react to his association of sneak attacks with Japan, he was disappointed. But I somehow felt he was simply speaking without self-editing.

"We had drive-bys even back then, is what I'm saying. Only that was *raiding,* not just blasting away. It takes real *cojones* to light up another gang's clubhouse. But if your club just rolled into enemy turf blasting out the windows at anything that moved, that'd bring your rep *down.*"

"Ah."

"You're supposed to get medals for killing the enemy, not for civilians. Why you think Ranger's so fucked in the head, Ho? We flew our colors like a flag, right out there where the enemy could see them. But Ranger, he didn't even know who the enemy *was.* Like he told us, they killed *plenty* of folks over there. Whole fucking villages. Just hosed 'em down, like those drive-by punks do now.

"I lost a pal behind that shit a few years ago. Everybody called him 'Pogo,' on account of he couldn't sit still. But he was a good pal; if he scored a dime, you had a nickel. Broad daylight, some motherfuckers just opened up on a little park downtown. Four people killed. Made all the papers—a little girl was shot in the head.

"I heard on the drums that Pogo was in the morgue. In the papers, they just said 'unidentified homeless man,' and some description that could fit half the niggers in this city. But I knew it was Pogo. Man never missed Wednesday suppers at this church in the Village. When he didn't show for two in a row, that was the same as Pogo's obituary. Only one he was ever going to get."

42

I had learned Lamont's story in pieces, as one slowly unwraps a precious gift. He had gone to prison as a young man for stabbing a rival gang leader in what another culture might have called a duel. Because his foe had died, Lamont's sentence had been a lengthy one.

While imprisoned, Lamont had taught himself to read. "You either kill the time or the time kills you," he told me, as if he needed to excuse what I viewed as a most admirable achievement.

Reading transported Lamont to places he had never known existed when he was "free." Through correspondence study, he became a college graduate, and looked forward to the day when he might become a teacher upon his release.

Such might have happened but for Lamont's poetry. Although truly gifted, he pursued his art for its own sake, quite content with the meager circulation his work received inside the closed circle of those with whom he corresponded.

This balance was disrupted when Lamont's poetry was somehow discovered by a wealthy woman with many literary connections. Her power was considerable, and Lamont's first volume of poetry, *B & E,* was published to great acclaim while he was still incarcerated.

"I thought I was going to be the next great thing, Ho," he told me. "I couldn't get over myself."

Arrogance as spirit-killer. This I understood.

"The minute I got the gate, I never looked back," Lamont continued. "I never looked at anything but my own picture on that book jacket. And I loved those literary parties—salons, they called them, Ho.

"But then I snapped that I wasn't a star; I was an exhibit in a traveling zoo. A petting zoo. 'Literary circle,' my ass. I was never one of them—I was just the fucking entertainment. They held me that high up just for the fun of stepping away and watching me crash.

"I'd faced death, Ho. And I had never blinked, not on the street, not in the joint. Death? I walked it down. Here's what I knew: if it took me, it'd be taking a *man*. When they poured that 'X' of red wine on the sidewalk and called my name, I'd hear it, wherever I was: 'Lamont, that boy, he had *heart.*'

"But those bloodsuckers did something to me I thought nobody could ever do. They *took* my heart, Ho."

That was the only time I ever saw Lamont surrender to his emotions. I stood guard as he sobbed. I was greatly honored to be entrusted with such a sacred task. I felt new power surge within me as I stood with my back to Lamont. None would see my friend in his moment of shame—I would die first. And it would be an honorable death.

43

Lamont has one copy of his book left. He carries it with him everywhere. The first time he allowed me to read it, I was plunged headlong down a mineshaft of empathetic loss. Lamont had written his own haiku. And it had been stolen from him.

44

"Got any ideas?" he asked me that morning.

"I do not," I confessed.

"I've been puzzling over it myself, Ho. There can't be

that many cars like the one we're looking for. But we don't exactly have access to the DMV computers, either."

"No," I agreed. "And a vehicle such as the one we seek would be garaged when not in use."

"So . . . ?"

"Would not such a car be driven by a chauffeur, rather than an individual?"

"Yeah . . ." Lamont said slowly, allowing his voice to trail off. "Unless . . ."

I waited as he took a generous sip from his cup. I noted that his eyes were clear and focused. Then I quickly reminded myself that I had often mistaken that look for sobriety.

"I keep thinking about the color, Ho."

"White? Does that have some special significance?"

"Maybe. It's kind of, I don't know . . . tacky, like. I mean, you're some kind of millionaire, maybe you want a Rolls to drive around in. *Be* driven around in, like you said. But white is just . . . *déclassé* for a car like that. White's for something you rent, not something you own."

"You think it might belong to a limousine company?"

"I *did* think that, for about a hot minute, but then something else came to me. Remember when Michael was describing the car?"

"Yes."

"He never said it was *big,*" Lamont said.

"Would that not be implied, considering the—"

"Sure, there's no such thing as a Rolls-Royce *compact,* that's right. But, Ho, if it was a stretch, that's something

Michael would have picked up on—that's from his world. His old world, I mean. The way I figure it, you're a limo company, you're going to invest in a damn *Rolls,* you go for the biggest one you can buy, get the most use out of it, see?"

"So we return to the idea of it being personally owned?"

"Right. Personally owned, personally driven. Who wants to make that kind of statement, Ho?"

I shrugged, indicating my lack of knowledge on the subject.

"A pimp," Lamont said, flatly. "If you're a pro athlete, or a rock star, or whatever, you get one of your posse to drive. But whoever heard of a pimp letting anyone besides himself behind the wheel of his ride?"

"I know nothing about such things," I acknowledged.

"The woman Michael saw, she was a *young* woman—"

"Michael did not say so," I protested.

"It's what he *didn't* say, Ho. If she had been an old lady—you know, the kind that's used to riding in the back seat—it would have been strange to see her climb out of the driver's seat. But Michael didn't say anything about that. And a *white* mink? That's a young broad's coat, not a dowager's."

"So you believe the young woman herself was a . . . ?"

"Hooker? That's right. And how is a hooker *ever* gonna be driving her pimp's car?"

"I do not understand how such things are done," I said. "If there is some sort of protocol—"

"We gotta get a newspaper, Ho," Lamont interrupted my unnecessarily defensive speech. "Not this morning, it's too soon. But maybe there'll be something about it later on."

"About . . . ?"

"A dead pimp," Lamont said, nodding to himself, as if confirming a complex proposition.

45

We strolled past a small vacant lot. *Temporarily* vacant, of course. Every square inch of ground is valuable here. New construction is as much a part of the fabric of this city as greed itself. It is immune to economic cycles, because it takes so many years to obtain the necessary permits that creating new luxury housing in the midst of economic disaster is commonplace.

A group of men and women were practicing t'ai chi, led by an elderly Chinese man dressed in a red jogging suit. His forms were quite good, but his transitions lacked the flow one would expect from a master of the art.

"You did stuff like that, right?" Lamont asked me.

"Something like it," I said. "Not the same."

We cut through an alley. As we reached the end, a large man with a shaved head spotted us. "Fucking nigger!" he shouted at Lamont.

We continued to walk toward the large man. "Fucking nigger!" he screamed again.

"You seeing things, man," Lamont said, grinning coldly. "I'm an albino."

The large man continued to scream his one phrase, but made no attempt to impede our progress.

In our world, such occurrences are commonplace.

46

"Perhaps the news might be on the radio?" I wondered out loud.

"Good call, Ho. Let's look for one."

Our search was not successful. Those establishments which had radios playing did not welcome those with no money to spend. We fished for a couple of hours to accumulate sufficient funds to enter a bodega and purchase a loaf of bread and a large bottle of apple juice. But even when we became paying customers, despite our most polite request, the proprietor refused to change the station on his radio.

The liquor store was also not accommodating. The man behind the thick curtain of bulletproof plastic recognized Lamont as a regular customer, but his only response was to repeat, "Buy something or get out," in a robotic, non-human tone.

We did not even consider trying one of the many coffeehouses that are sprinkled throughout the neighborhood. We knew from experience that those who inhabit such places might fervently advocate for "The Homeless" when conversing among themselves, but would not continue to patronize any place that allowed us to loiter. Owners would advertise this policy in a variety of ways, the most common being a sign warning that use of the bathrooms was reserved for customers.

By early afternoon, the landscape was overpowered by the sun, bleaching rather than beautifying. Lamont and I turned our steps toward a tiny decrepit cement park that might once have been used by children.

"*That's* what we want," Lamont said, pointing out a group of teenagers lounging at the base of a decapitated statue. The object of his attention was a large radio, the kind with speakers attached to its sides by wires.

As we moved closer, the noise from the speakers became as violently intrusive as a jackhammer, albeit less musical.

The young people showed no wariness at our approach. This was not due to any soporific drugs they may have consumed, or a deliberate pose adopted to demonstrate indifference. As Lamont never tired of repeating, those not from our world simply do not *see* us.

"Hey, brother," Lamont greeted a young black man with beaded dreadlocks who stood on the fringe of the group. "Me and my partner wonder, could we ask you to dial your box for a few minutes? There's something we need to listen to on the radio, bro."

"What's that, man?" the youth replied. "The stock quotes?"

His wit was rewarded with a palm slap from a white teenager dressed in a grossly oversized shirt with the number 23 on it, hanging down over extremely baggy pants that did not fully cover his ankles.

"I ain't asking to *hold* the box, bro. Just to listen for five, ten minutes," Lamont wheedled, almost servilely. "Means nothing to you; could mean a lot to us."

"Thing is, *you* don't mean nothing to me," the black youth said, glancing around to be certain the others understood how well he was playing the role he had chosen for himself.

Whether the others fully comprehended this, I could not

know. But I remembered Lamont's lesson: when seeking something from another, always allow him to preserve his image. So I approached the dreadlocked youth as if he were a man of power and importance. In his world, "getting paid" would be a hallmark of such a position.

"Perhaps we might *rent* the use of your radio?" I offered, humbly.

"Yeah? For what, a bag of aluminum cans?" the black youth said, drawing the obligatory laughter from the group that had assembled around us.

"Certainly not," I said, as if I had better manners than to expect a man of his stature to accept trivial offerings. "Would, say, ten dollars suffice?" I asked.

"You *got* ten dollars, old man?"

"We do not," I told him honestly. "But we will pledge that amount to you, and return with it as soon as we have earned it."

His group reacted as if I had been seeking their contempt, two of them nearly convulsing with laughter.

I felt no anger, only sadness that the concept of a man keeping his word was so alien to them that it would inspire hilarity. I stepped back, having nothing more to offer. But Lamont was not so easily deterred.

"I read you, bro," Lamont said. "But no cash don't make us trash. So how about if we trade you, instead? A little magic for a little dial time?"

"Magic?" a young girl with spiked purple hair immediately responded.

"Magic," Lamont solemnly confirmed. He pointed at a medium-height, very muscular youth, whose only upper garment was a yellow sleeveless shirt. "You go, what, about two twenty?"

"Pretty close," the muscular young man said, folding his arms to emphasize his biceps.

"Bench, what, four fifty, four seventy-five?"

"So what?" the young man said, not acknowledging that Lamont had overestimated his lifting capacity by a considerable amount.

"So this, bro. *Magic!* I say, even those big guns you're packing, you still can't move my partner here."

"The old man?"

"Yeah," Lamont said, his teeth forming an ice-smile that went unrecognized by the younger man. "I'm saying, you can't budge him an *inch,* okay? My man, he got *powers.* All he has to do is say this spell he knows, and he can root himself right to the ground, like he was a tree."

"Lamont . . ." I said, very softly. But it was too late.

"I can't move *this* old man?" the heavily muscled youth said, jabbing a stiffened forefinger at my shoulder. I flowed with his gesture, so that his finger felt only the illusion of contact.

"Magic," Lamont answered calmly. "Ten bucks' worth."

The muscular youth did not reply. Instead, he grabbed my coat in his fists and rammed his shoulder into my chest. I turned into his thrust using an ebb-and-flow technique, being careful not to move my feet.

"Fuck!" the youth said.

"This will not work," I cautioned Lamont.

"You motherfucking right it won't work," the youth said, grimly, as if to announce to the others that his earlier attempt had not been in earnest.

“Whoa, bro! You don’t get to play for free,” Lamont told the young man, loudly enough so that all in the vicinity could hear.

“Knock him on his ass!” the dreadlocked leader authorized.

Instantly, the muscular youth’s features contorted, announcing his strike well before he committed to it. I transformed the energy of his awkward punch so that his face was urged to become one with the concrete.

But when I looked up, I saw that instead of honoring their agreement the others had fled . . . taking their radio with them.

Only the girl with the purple-spiked hair remained. I recognized the look on her face, so I locked Lamont’s arm against my body and walked him rapidly out of the park.

“Why must you constantly do such things?” I asked him.

“Hey, Ho, that wasn’t me; it was him. His desire to do you an injury is what injured him, right?”

I bowed slightly, accepting that Lamont was mocking that part of me I had yet to fully cleanse.

“And yet we still have no radio,” I pointed out, gently.

“Plenty of rounds left in the clip,” Lamont replied, undiscouraged. In fact, he seemed to be enjoying himself.

47

Brewster’s library is on the top floor of a building that was once an arsonist’s playground. The interior first-floor walls have crumbled, leaving only a single huge room which has become a public toilet.

Even the most desperate of our tribe would not venture to sleep in such a place. The first floor is urban quicksand—human waste alive with voracious rats. And the only remaining stairway to other floors is not trustworthy, its slimy treacherousness amplified by the ever-present darkness.

Brewster has contrived to make the passage to the highest floor—the fourth—even more difficult, by use of strands of razor wire purloined from construction sites. He knows that none who enter the building would be seeking anything more than a place to relieve themselves, aware that the price of sleep could be death. Nevertheless, Brewster must be absolutely *certain* his treasures are safe in his absence—even the thick bales of rat poison that line the space he uses are constantly refreshed.

As a further precaution, all Brewster's paperback books are carefully sealed inside multiple layers of plastic storage bags.

Maintaining his library is hard labor; Brewster's diligence to his task is remarkable. I was impressed by the extent of his precautions, especially in regard to personal hygiene. Each time he enters the building, Brewster carries a complete change of clothing inside several thick trash bags. When he exits, he removes all his fouled clothing and throws it away. Then he cleanses his body with antiseptic wipes, and changes into the clothing he brought with him.

Even though Brewster can accomplish all this at amazing speed, he has twice been apprehended by the police while still in a state of undress. Apparently—I do not actually understand how this works—Brewster carries certain identification that allows him to avoid arrest on such occasions.

Although Brewster acquires his books only by honest means, be they purchase or laborious scavenging, his personal code allows him to shoplift anything required to maintain them. The book-storage bags he uses are apparently sold in numerous comic-book stores throughout the city. Brewster is a very successful shoplifter, because he always presents a neat, clean appearance and is unfailingly polite. Additionally, he does make occasional purchases, so his "browsing" is not viewed with suspicion.

Lamont explained that Brewster's "no fall" history is due to the fact that such stores will zealously guard their most expensive merchandise, but pay no real attention to trivial items such as storage bags.

Michael and Ranger had once managed to procure several large cartons of these plastic bags. I do not know how they achieved this, although it was clear they had meshed their respective skills to collaborate on the project. Brewster was almost overcome with gratitude. Michael was quite proud of the achievement, but provided no details. Ranger was silent.

"I just hope that psycho didn't ice some delivery guy," Lamont had whispered to me at the time.

Brewster's older sister allows him to visit her home whenever he wishes. Each time, he returns with fresh clothing, and small amounts of money. He can visit only in the daytime; his sister's husband objects to his presence.

None of us has ever asked him why he chooses to live our life.

For many years, Brewster was able to spend every night in his library. Inevitably, his collection grew so that it took up all the available space, and he was never insane enough to try sleeping downstairs. Now any agreement to "meet at Brewster's library" actually signifies that we will assemble outside the building. From there, we move as one until we find a place to discuss whatever is necessary.

That evening, immediately upon his arrival, I noticed that Michael was wearing a new pair of running shoes. "New" as in "different," to be more precise. Between the privileged joggers who fervently believe such gear must be replaced every few months, and the sheep who would rather suffer physical pain than be seen wearing out-of-fashion footwear, the Dumpsters throughout the city provide a steady supply for those of our tribe.

Outwardly, Ranger was dressed as he always is, but his body posture spoke clearly to me.

"Did we not agree there would be no weapons?" I said, taking care to phrase it as a question, not a command.

"But, Ho, we're on a mission," Ranger said, plaintively.

"An *undercover* mission," I reminded him. "And the presence of weapons might compromise our position if the police were to . . . intervene."

Ranger reluctantly nodded agreement. Somehow, his brain had retained sufficient cognitive function to process the fact that his intermittent hospital stays were always greatly extended when preceded by a weapons charge. He extracted a large, formidable-looking knife from his coat and handed it to me.

"That's a Ka-Bar," Lamont said, whistling. "Looks brand-new, too. Got a sheath for it, Ranger?"

"Roger!" he replied, producing a complicated-looking black nylon harness.

"Now, this, this is *exactly* what we've been looking for!" Lamont said, excitedly.

"A knife?" Brewster asked, puzzled.

"Knife! Life! Wife! Strife!" Target muttered.

"I can get us a *sweet* radio for this," Lamont vowed. "With plenty of batteries, too. Have to go uptown, though."

The others listened closely as I explained Lamont's theory that the car we sought might have belonged to a pimp. "A dead pimp," Lamont added. I watched Michael's eyes flare with gambler's lust, but he remained silent.

Once it became clear that a radio was vital to our mission, all agreed that we should do whatever was necessary to obtain one, and that Lamont should be entrusted with the task.

Michael and Brewster understood they could not accompany Lamont. Their understandings came via different channels, but reached to the same depth. Ranger saw obtaining the radio as a "one-man job." Target is capable of attaching himself to any of us, but only when at least one more is present. Two is a number he fears.

In addition to his new shoes, the day's fishing had gone well for Michael. This even though Ranger had never left his side, which usually creates a significant handicap. There was enough money for us all to eat a healthy meal of noodles and rice. It had taken me a very long time to wean the group away from the filthy, chemically processed foods they had previously preferred. But now the eating habits had become part of our band's culture, an accepted fact of life. Several Japanese restaurants in our part of the city had come to expect my periodic appearances.

Whenever we decided on a variation—Korean, say, or Vietnamese—Brewster or Michael would be sent in to make the purchase. It is another comic-book myth that all Asians consider themselves brothers. The truth is quite the contrary. Although being able to converse in Japanese had undoubtedly produced larger portions of food in some of the take-out places we frequent, it would have a distinctly adverse effect were the proprietor to be Chinese.

Dividing our food never presents a problem. Ranger is in charge of this, and believes that troops should share their rations in the field. He is meticulously fair, to the point of self-denial, and is trusted unequivocally. By now, all of us are passably competent with chopsticks, but Target is by far the most adept.

48

When Lamont rejoined us later that night, it was nine minutes past one o'clock. Ranger announced the time.

"I had to keep this sucker under wraps," Lamont said, as he removed a small portable radio from under the black wool overcoat he wears year-round.

As we all visually admired his acquisition, Lamont proudly demonstrated how the radio had multiple bands, accessible via its extendable antenna. "You can pick up the BBC on this little jewel easy as the local weather," he told us, pointing out various listening options as he spoke.

"You did well," I told him.

"Goddamn right!" Michael agreed.

Ranger had not spoken. Lamont reached in his coat pocket, and handed him something.

"What's that?" Brewster asked.

"It's a . . . compass, man!" Ranger said, temporarily overcome with emotions he has long since lost the ability to comprehend. "Damn! I *needed* one of these. Thanks, Lamont!"

That was the first time I ever heard Ranger call Lamont by name.

We listened to our radio throughout the night. The city has several "all-news" stations, and we alternated among them. Several different homicides were reported, but none remotely matched the criteria we sought.

"Maybe they don't know yet," Michael finally said. "I mean, say she killed him indoors—the body could stay there for days without anyone discovering it, especially if she turned the air conditioning way up."

"And that car would be hot," Brewster chimed in. "So she'd want to keep it off the streets."

"Sweep the ville!" Ranger volunteered.

"It would seem there might be too many houses," I pointed out, spreading my arms to indicate the vastness of the city, as if this were the only impediment to his psychotic suggestion.

"I'll keep monitoring the news," Lamont promised, showing us a small bag full of batteries. "And we can check the papers, too."

"How about we put it on the grapevine?" Brewster said, speaking out of the side of his mouth.

Michael, who refuses to accept that Brewster's every word is some sort of re-enactment of the books to which he is addicted, immediately said, "No!" I noted the unnecessary sharpness of his tone. "This is *ours,*" Michael said, pointing his finger as if accusing Brewster of betrayal. "If people get the idea that car's worth something, you think they're going to come back to *us* if they spot it?"

"Man's telling it true." Lamont supported Michael—another uncommon occurrence. "We gotta keep this to ourselves. Remember, we're holding aces. We're the only ones who know. And we got nothing *but* time."

49

Several days passed without incident. Each of us waited, each in his own way.

One especially fine day, Lamont and I were anticipating Brewster's arrival—he had promised to bring some fresh batteries for our radio. The early-afternoon sun was still strong, and we relaxed under its soothing warmth. Our pleasure was enriched by the knowledge that the sun's blessing was distributed without regard to status.

"I got them!" Brewster announced his arrival. True to his word, he had three packets of batteries, still in their plastic seals.

"You did well," I told him.

"I found out something else, too!" he burst out. "This is really important, Ho."

"Yes?" I said.

Lamont took another drink from his paper bag.

"I went to the library," Brewster said. "The big one, on Forty-second. You know what Michael's always saying, you can find *anything* there? So I figured I'd check the papers from other cities. Ones close to here, I mean, like over in Jersey. Maybe there would be something in there about a dead pimp. Or a missing Rolls-Royce."

I said nothing. Lamont took another sip of whatever was in his paper bag.

"But there wasn't anything, okay?" Brewster continued. "So I figured, as long as I'm there, I should see what they have on Rolls-Royces. I mean, like . . . research."

Again, I did not speak. Again, Lamont's response was to sip his elixir.

"You know what I found out, Ho? They only make a few of them every year, and they don't sell most of them here. In America, I mean. The new ones, they're called 'Phantoms.' That's not just the make; that's the model. Like, there's all different kinds of Fords—you know, like, say a Ford Focus or a Ford Crown Vic—but not for them. Rolls-Royce, I mean."

"That seems—"

"Nah, my man's on the *case,* Ho," Lamont said. He turned to Brewster, asked, "You mean, all the ones you could drive yourself around in, those are Phantoms, right?"

"Yeah!" Brewster said, even more excited by Lamont's reference to him as "my man" than by his reaction to the "research."

"And the ones you saw, the Phantoms, they all had tops?"

"Well, sure . . ."

"I mean, like, *hard* tops." Lamont was encouraging Brewster's initiative, for reasons I did not understand. "There's no Phantom convertibles?"

"Deduction," Brewster said solemnly, tapping his temple. "But here's the really important thing about them." He paused dramatically, then lowered his voice before saying, "They don't *come* in white!"

"There are no white . . . 'Phantoms'?" I asked gently, exchanging a look with Lamont.

"They don't come in white," Brewster repeated. "You know what that means?"

"No," I said, speaking honestly.

"Means, who's gonna be slapping a paint job on a *Rolls*?" Lamont explained to me.

"Because that would be . . . superfluous?" I asked.

Lamont and Brewster exchanged a glance before saying, "A pimp!" in a single voice. Lamont's real world and Brewster's fictional one intersected at that moment, as if synapses had connected in the same brain.

50

That two such disparate minds had reached the same conclusion did not create a solution. Weeks passed without a single mention of a murdered pimp in any of the media accessible to us. Though this in no way dampened the enthusiasm of Michael and Ranger, who continued to fuel each other's fire, our treasure map was growing more tarnished with every passing day.

“I think Brewster gave us the true clue,” Lamont said to me one night.

“About the car being repainted?”

“No, Ho. When he said what they were called—those kind of cars, I mean. The way I thought it might have gone down, that was a shot in the dark. We’re spinning our wheels, I think.”

“You mean we have no traction?”

“People like us, we never have traction,” Lamont said, the poet in his soul overcoming his streetwise persona. “Life ain’t nothing but a roulette wheel. Everybody gets a spin, but we don’t all get to spin the same wheel. It don’t matter where the ball drops when all the numbers are zeros.”

“So locating this car is a gamble we could never win?” I asked, attempting to translate Lamont’s metaphors.

“No, bro. Folks *do* hit the lottery, right? It can happen if it *can* happen.”

“I do not—”

“I think we’ve all been looking for a phantom, Ho. Just like Brewster said. Only not some car’s name, a phantom for real.”

“You mean, like, a ghost?”

“Yeah, brother. *Just* like that. The way I see it, we’re looking for something that was never there to begin with. And while we doing that, the one real thing we got—Brewster’s library, I mean—it’s slipping away. The man’s running out of room.”

51

Hours passed in silence. Without so much as exchanging a look, we arose as one and began to walk.

Neither of us spoke.

Hours later, we reached my shrine. We stood across the street from a magnificent limestone building, an ornate structure that proclaimed its craftsmanship and solidity, as if to distance itself from those chrome-and-glass boxes which dominate the city's skyline.

On the third anniversary of Chica's death, a series of events had occurred within that building, events as mysterious and inexplicable as a group of insane individuals executing a demonstration of perfect teamwork.

The chain began when a man in some sort of Army jacket lit the rag wick of a glass bottle filled with gasoline and soap chips, screamed "Incoming!" and threw it at the entrance to the building. The man immediately disappeared into the night, as if his mission had been completed.

When the doorman ran out to investigate, a large black man staggered into his path, drunk and hostile, demanding money.

As the doorman attempted to extricate himself from the black man's drunken embrace, an individual clad in a black bodysuit with a yellow skeleton drawn on it charged into the lobby. The creature's face was covered with an orange Halloween mask; he carried a large can of black spray paint in each gloved hand. The security cameras recorded him shrieking in rage as he madly sprayed each lens into blindness. Had their audio been sufficient, they might have recorded a string of rhyming epithets—"Bad! Mad! Sad! Dad!"—as the skeleton fled.

As the doorman was shouting at the drunk never to come back around *his* building again or he would summon the police, an elderly man slipped inside unseen, tapped each of the four elevators to summon them down to the first floor, and began the climb to the penthouse, using the stairs.

The stairway was well lit, but apparently never used by the building's residents. The man moved from shadow to shadow without difficulty, for he had become one himself.

Chica's stepfather answered the doorbell. The gods were gracious that night—he was alone in his apartment.

52

The following morning, the newspapers reported that Chica's stepfather had either leapt or fallen from his private balcony to the street below. One of his friends speculated that the stress of his long-running lawsuit—he had sued Chica's mother for libel and slander—had taken a terrible toll on him.

An autopsy revealed alcohol in his blood at the time of death, but the coroner said the amount was considerably short of the legal standard for intoxication.

Although he left no note, the death of Chica's stepfather was eventually ruled a suicide. Because he had been alone the night he plunged into the welcoming blackness, no other explanation fit the known facts.

53

As we stood together in the approaching darkness, Lamont ceremoniously handed me a tiny, corked bottle of sake, then unscrewed the cap on a much larger bottle of clear liquid. Uniting our traditions, together we poured an invisible "X" onto the concrete, which I then set ablaze with a wooden match.

54

One night—I know it will come in the night—I will finally be free to depart this world. Only then will I be able to offer my haiku to Chica.

Until then, I struggle to make it worthy of the spirit I must become before I may apologize.

Obstacles lie in the path of attaining my spirit. I have no fear of them, but for one.

Time.

55

It is said that the true meaning of Hell is the knowledge that there is a depth yet below, and what was floor may become ceiling.

This is truth. The most wretched of this earth are those who know there is always something worse yet to come.

The worst despair of all is to accept the inevitability of further descent. In the utter blackness of such a pit, any door marked "Exit" will be opened, eagerly and blindly.

Some choose hope. Michael's "mortal lock" dream is his shield, just as the belief that sufferers will be rewarded in some mystical Afterlife shields others.

Some renounce hope. Ranger knows he will die in battle. This does not frighten him; it comforts him.

Lamont maintains total faith in his ability to "roll with" whatever might occur.

Target cannot envision tomorrow—he has the immunity of the truly insane.

Only Brewster had failed to develop an internal defense of his own.

56

"It's all coming down," Brewster told us that humid summer night. "Everything. Everything's all coming down."

He spoke as carefully as a man defusing a bomb, as if he realized any display of emotion could be fatal. Each of his words was a separate, measured entity. His lips barely moved. His body was so rigid that it vibrated—any sudden movement could shatter him as easily as a dry twig in the hands of a curious monkey.

Lamont instantly deduced that only one thing could reduce Brewster to such a state. He patted the air in front of him, signaling us all to silence.

"You sure?" is all he asked.

"The sign is there," Brewster said. His voice was mechanical, purely a transmitter of information.

"Let's check it out," Lamont said.

We moved in silence, surrounding Brewster as we proceeded. "Point," Ranger hissed, as he slid into position so that he would be the first one of us anyone would encounter. Following his silent commands, I slid to the back, Lamont and Michael each walked alongside of Brewster. Target orbited around us.

57

The sign was there. And it was just that: a sign, not an omen requiring interpretation. Its meaning was as literal as Brewster's speech had been.

Lamont's forecast that soon there would be no room left in Brewster's library was now moot. The building that housed Brewster's library was marked for demolition. A "Total Green Technology" twelve-unit condominium was to be erected in its place.

The sign informed all that a prospectus was available for review, as well as architectural renderings and a "cyber-tour." The new building's "open" design would allow for "individual personalization" of each unit by its purchaser.

Demolition was to commence in three months.

For Brewster, it *was* all coming down. The floor of his personal Hell had suddenly opened beneath his feet.

58

"Move out!" Ranger commanded. "Soon as it gets light, this is gonna be a hot LZ."

We walked all the way to the pier without exchanging another word, Brewster always in the center of our protective diamond, carried along by the waves of our motion. As we moved, I deliberately avoided contemplation of the task facing us. My immediate concern was protection of our moving band—and any loss of concentration would diminish my abilities.

But even on full alert, some part of my mind could not help wondering how Ranger knew that remaining next to Brewster's building might cause the young man to disintegrate. Or had he perceived danger of another kind, one that might pose a threat to us all?

I banished this thought by recalling the words of one of my teachers. "If you ask, 'Why is this man attempting to injure me?' you create a space within which his weapon may enter. Analysis is proper *before* combat, so that a strategy may be formulated. Analysis is proper *following* combat, so that one may refine technique and correct mistakes. But analysis *during* combat invades focus. And whatever robs you of focus always aids your attacker."

59

Seated in a circle under the pier, we all looked to Lamont.

"We gotta move my man's stash," he summarized our task. It prompted a "Stash! Bash! Crash! Trash!" outburst from Target that we all ignored.

"We need the specs," Ranger said.

"It's all books," Michael told him.

"Ranger knows it's all books," I interrupted, recognizing the slight shift in Ranger's shoulders that always accompanied any perception that he was being mocked. "His question was quite reasonable. We have to move objects. How can we do this without knowing the total size and weight?"

"How are we supposed to—?"

"Brewster knows," Lamont cut Michael off. He turned to the young man, said: "Give us the numbers, bro."

Brewster slowly rotated his head to face Lamont, his frozen mask flexing only slightly.

"Dimensions," Michael explained, switching from his earlier sarcasm to sympathy as if the former had never existed. "You know your books, Brewster. Maybe they're not all the same size, but if we had some basic info, we could work it out."

"Are all your books not somewhat similar in size?" I asked, very gently.

"Dies! Rise! Prize! Lies!"

The last word of Target's string triggered something within Brewster. His posture grew less rigid. Lamont handed him a cigarette, no small gift in our world. He was aware that smoking always brought Brewster closer to the world of his books.

Brewster took the cigarette, still moving stiffly. But when he said, "Thanks, pal," to Lamont, we could see he was going to return to us.

Lamont struck a match, cupping it carefully. There was no wind, but both Ranger—who does not smoke—and Brewster were adamant about shielding any such flame. Brewster took a deep drag, and nodded in satisfaction as he channeled one of the protagonists in his sacred books.

"The library is all paperbacks," he said, talking out of

the side of his mouth. "Not the crap they sell now, reprints. These're all paperback *originals,* see?"

Lamont nodded his approval, whether of Brewster's starting to talk or because of some philosophical agreement with his "old school" standard, I could not tell.

"They're all approximately four inches wide by seven inches tall," Brewster said, with the self-assurance of a man stepping out of a quagmire onto concrete. "Depth varies, but somewhere between one-half and three-quarters of an inch. A lot of them are even thinner."

"They're in those bag things, though, right? To protect them?"

"You got it," Brewster answered Michael.

"All right, we have to figure that adds *something*. Say we round it off to three-quarters of an inch apiece. So how many are we talking about here?"

"Four thousand, seven hundred, and twenty-nine," Brewster answered without a pause.

"A little under three hundred running feet," Michael said, just as quickly. "Weight?"

"Under five ounces, all of them."

"Maxes to three quarters of a ton," Michael shot back. "Figuring we have to box them up for transport, probably brings it closer to one ton, total."

"Got boys all over this city driving those dumbass pickup trucks like they live on a fucking farm," Lamont mused.

"You move ordnance, you draw fire," Ranger warned.

"This ain't no—" Lamont began, before catching my warning look, and smoothly ending his sentence with: "—job for a pickup. What we need is a van. Not one of those soccer-mom things, something like they use to deliver things."

"Who delivers at two in the morning?" Michael said, as if we had already agreed that deep darkness was an essential element of our plan.

"We don't want to draw fire," Ranger repeated, his voice hardening.

"Sure. But we wouldn't be exposed long. If we tried it in daylight and we had to go crosstown, we could be sitting ducks," Michael pointed out.

"Flowers!" Lamont said.

"Showers! Towers! Hours! Powers!" Target erupted. But instead of ignoring him, we all turned in his direction. For the first time any of us had ever observed, Target was clanging in a barely audible whisper, instead of his usual shouting or angry muttering.

"The flower joints on Second, they're all open at like four in the morning," Lamont said. "Open for deliveries, I mean—they gotta have *fresh,* they want to stay in business. I don't know where they pick up from, but those flower vans, they run all over the Lower West Side, every night."

"Capacity!" Ranger barked.

Silence reigned. When it became obvious that Ranger was not going to amplify his statement, I spoke as if responding to the question I believed he had asked.

"That is a most valid point to consider," I said. "Michael has given us a perfect calculation of weight, but it is not as if we are moving a one-ton brick—everything must fit inside whatever we use, because we will not have more than a single opportunity to relocate Brewster's library."

"Cubic feet," Michael said.

I nodded.

"None of that's a secret," Michael went on. "The library will have all the specs."

"Job One," Ranger confirmed. It required no translator to understand this. That we had no place to store a stolen van—much less the cargo we intended to transport in it—was less important than making certain we obtained the correct vehicle in the first place.

"Tomorrow?" I asked.

"First thing," Michael promised.

60

Those of our tribe quickly learn that sleep, which rests and refreshes those in the other world, brings little comfort to us. Sleep means exposure to danger, both the mind and the body open to attack. So we rise early, and we stay in motion, resting only when necessary.

Some regard this adaptation as a survival tool. Ranger will refuse sleep entirely unless we all agree to take turns on watch. Some become so highly amped that they are susceptible to sudden onsets of unconsciousness, as if an unseen switch had been thrown. Michael calls this "crashing," and tells us he saw it occur many times during his life on Wall Street. Target is also prone to this. But, unlike Michael, he is terrified of the prospect, which is why he cannot bear to be alone.

Only Lamont is utterly indifferent. Awake, he displays a finely tuned balance: neither an easy target nor a threat worthy of challenge. Asleep, he projects the same *ki*.

As I age, I find I need sleep less each year.

But each time I close my eyes, it is with the silent prayer that I not dream.

So, early that morning, Ranger was on a scouting mission, presumably for an unguarded van; Michael was waiting for the public library to open; and Lamont and I were visually appraising the task we had accepted.

Target was with us. Perhaps it was his sudden switch to whispering the previous night that made me look closer, but it seemed to me that his movements were now markedly less spasmodic than I had ever observed.

Brewster was at his sister's, the sand draining from his hourglass.

61

"Light stuff," Lamont said to me. "Between us, we got all the skills we need to crack this crib."

"Do we?" I asked, in the tone of one seeking to confirm the assurance Lamont was offering.

"Come on, Ho. I was just a young buck when they took me down on my last bit, but that warlord stuff never paid the rent. Me, I was an ace burglar. And you, you're like a ninja, right?"

"A burglar is a thief," I reminded Lamont.

"What're you saying?"

"The skill in burglary is to take items of value without being detected, yes?"

"Sure. But—"

"The finest burglar should be able to bypass any security

system, enter the area, remove whatever he sought, and not leave a trace of his presence."

"Man, I could do *all* that, bro. Learned from the best. One time, I slipped in a window—you know how it gets in the summer around here; back then, lots of folks didn't have no A/C, always left the windows open at night—and there was this woman, sound asleep. Now, if I was one of those sickos, I'd've said, 'Damn! This one's ripe for the taking.' And if I was an amateur, I'd've just split. But me, I went about my business. Professional. Got some decent stuff, filled my bag, and went back out the same way I came in. That woman, she never even woke up."

I bowed in respectful acknowledgment of the skills he had described. Then I said, "But, Lamont, there is no security to defeat in Brewster's library. And the goods we need to remove will not fit into a bag any man could carry."

"Okay . . ." Lamont paused, then said, "What about you, Ho? I mean, a ninja—"

"A ninja is an assassin," I told my friend.

Lamont took a long drink from the large plastic cup he was holding. He closed his eyes in concentration.

"Brewster got them *up* there," he said, thoughtfully.

I said nothing.

"But that was, what, three, four at a time? Took him years to stuff that place to the brim."

Again, I waited.

"When I was Upstate, there was a white guy who *ruled* the joint. More of us than them, even back then, but the white boys saw it coming before we did. So, even when we all got 'conscious,' it didn't hold us together.

"Never mind that East Coast–West Coast thing the Panthers had going—even the fucking *Muslims* were splitting up and shanking each other. The PRs could have had the whole thing, the way they were pouring in. *Seasoned* guys, too. Young, maybe, but already blooded. You'd think, Inside, they'd stop flying their colors, get down with their race. Not a chance; motherfuckers stayed as stupid as we were. So busy jacking each other, it's like we all *made* the white boys stick together."

Lamont took another drink. I waited for him to return from wherever he had gone. His eyes blinked rapidly, as if he were awakening from sleep, but he snapped into focus as if he had never left:

"So, anyway, like I was saying, when I first got there, the wheel—this white guy—he had a ton of swag. Mostly cigarettes, commissary stuff, fuck-and-suck books . . . anything you could juggle—"

My raised eyebrows were a long-established method of interrupting Lamont when I did not understand his terminology.

"Juggling is like loan-sharking, Ho. Guy's got no smokes, okay? You let him take a couple of crates. Next month, he's got to come up with three to pay you back, see?"

I nodded.

"So I'm saying, this guy had so much stuff in his house that he couldn't even get to his bunk, never mind the toilet."

"How did he solve that problem?"

"Juice," Lamont said. "The wheel, he was connected outside, too. Can't be greasing the hacks with cigarettes. Those dumbass farm boys they hired probably never even saw a nigger until they started working in the joint, but they learned quick—all they wanted was cash. Take care of them, they take care of you."

"So the guards were bribed?"

"Every day," Lamont said. "You could buy anything in there you could buy on the streets. Except pussy. And you could even get *that* on Visiting Day . . . provided you had the long green. The hacks'd let you take a woman into one of the bathrooms, even stand watch outside. It was like bonus pay for them."

"So much money? Inside a prison?"

"Nah. Soft money—actual cash in your hand, not money on the books—that's a real bad ticket. Only reason you'd want cash is if you were planning to go for the Wall. You get caught holding some, you're looking at *years* in the bing. Solitary, okay?"

"Then . . . ?"

"It's a different economy, Ho. Say a guy wants a deck of H, how's he gonna get it? From another con, right? Lots of ways to pay that got nothing to do with cash. Question is, how's the con you buy from get *his* supply?"

"The guards bring it in."

"Bingo. But they get *paid* on the outside. Cash in an envelope. The Mafia guys, they had that all rigged. But that wasn't the only way. One guy I remember, big-time pimp: man had so much game that his girls were *still* out there working for him. That's money. Gang men—men like me—your boys would be looking out for you. Some guys had wives who could come up with the tolls. It was known which of the hacks would take some. One greedy motherfucker even had his own damn PO box!

"Later on, when the dope game really hit, there was more cash out there than you could ever imagine. The white guys couldn't hold us off—we were getting a bigger and bigger piece all the time. Even the Latins were getting theirs. Money, money, money. And the hacks were making more from the cons than they were from the State.

"Take booze. If you were an off-brand—no gang connect—you had to stick with pruno . . . home brew. But if you could reach out, you'd be drinking bonded whiskey. A little portable radio might cost a hack thirty bucks, but it'd cost a con a couple a hundred, see?"

"And everyone knew—?"

"Oh, *hell,* yes!" Lamont said. "Just like when a dirty cop rolls up a dealer and finds out he's packing a fat wad. You think that cop's lieutenant isn't getting a piece of that score? And the captain, too?

"That's just the way it was. Even when one of the hacks got caught, it was no big deal. Except for bringing in a gun—for that, they'd drop the hammer. But if you needed a twenty-two bullet for a little zip you made, no problem."

"So this man with the crammed-full cell . . . ?"

"Oh, they just put him in the cell next door to that one. Motherfucker had him *two* private cells, while they were double-bunking other poor bastards all over the joint."

"Yes," I said. "But such solutions are not available to us."

"'Cause we don't have the coin?" Lamont drawled, in a sleepy voice I knew was no indication of his actual mental state. "Well, you know how people say you can always make money? They don't mean you can print it up—not saying plenty haven't tried, though—they mean you can work for it, right? Where I'm from, the way you *make* money is, you *take* money."

"Fake! Shake! Cake! Trafe!" Target whispered.

"Let's see what's out back," Lamont said.

62

We had never previously explored the area around Brewster's library. Those of our tribe own nothing we cannot carry, so we do not concern ourselves with defending space as others do. For us, the most desirable feature of any place we might occupy would be ease of exit.

That was what caused the initial resistance to construction of our dugout sleeping quarters on the pier. In a world where some will kill to acquire what others have discarded, *all* things have value. Those who desperately sought shelter on the street itself were always on display, looked down upon from glass boxes as if the pantomime of poverty was some form of performance art. But we were not trapped in our dugouts, we were invisible.

The original resistance to the dugouts had come only from Michael and Brewster.

Michael had once been torn from under a shelter he had constructed of cardboard and wood, by a madman who beat him with a lead pipe so severely that only the fortuitous passing of a police car had saved his life. Brewster had no actual experience with violence, but the catechism of his paperbacks taught him, "You always gotta know where the back door is."

Brewster rarely spent his nights with us. His fresh-faced appearance, his newly laundered clothing, and the fact that he possessed a full set of identification allowed him to sleep in public places we could not even visit. If questioned by the police, he would act as if his medication had caused drowsiness. Since he did not touch alcohol, he gave off no contrary signals. Brewster told us he had never been arrested.

Michael's fears were eventually mollified by Ranger's assurances that he could catch the scent of approaching enemies at a great distance, and could hear the softest of footsteps in his sleep. Michael was also aware that Lamont is physically quite capable, and that I myself am never defenseless.

Target's only fear is to be alone. If we walk away, he follows; if we stay, he stays.

63

Exploring the area for the first time, we discovered that behind Brewster's library was a narrow alley, separating the backs of two different sets of buildings.

"Wide enough for a garbage truck," Lamont observed, noting the various green metal Dumpsters marked with the name of a private carting firm.

We walked the length of the alley in the early sunlight, not surprised to find it unoccupied. The Dumpsters would already have been emptied, and those who scour them for nourishment—human and otherwise—would not return until after the food establishments closed for the night. In this part of the city, it is not uncommon to find an exclusive restaurant next to a tiny storefront dispensing cheap, near-rancid take-out. Michael explained that such establishments would disappear as soon as their leases expired.

"This one," Lamont said, stopping behind a four-story building. All the glass was gone from the windows, so there was no barrier to the elements. The sole exception was some plywood-and-plastic sheeting covering two windows on the top floor.

Lamont turned his back on Brewster's building. I followed his example. The building we faced was two stories taller, and obviously occupied.

Several minutes passed.

"Got it," Lamont said, as if he had just solved a complex problem.

64

The electronic clock in the window of a stately bank told us we still had over two hours to acquire money for food before meeting Michael and Ranger. But since our meeting was to be in an area near the Hudson River, across from what is known as the Meatpacking District, we had a considerable distance to travel as well.

We always use that same place for pre-arranged meetings if they are to occur in daylight. At night, it is clogged with prostitutes of all genders. Cars drive through slowly, like suburban housewives pushing their carts through the aisles of a supermarket. But both predators and prey react to sunlight like vampires, so we are able to sit and have a meal together with very little chance of being disturbed.

"No time for fishing, Ho," Lamont said. "Got to score a double-sawbuck at least."

"No 'magic,'" I warned him.

"Fantastic! Tragic! Statistic! Sadistic!" Target erupted.

A part of my mind pondered—not for the first time—whether Target's extensive vocabulary was a sign that his clanging had a specific sequence. Was what we regarded as the reaction of a damaged mind to certain stimuli actually an attempt to communicate?

Such thoughts came to me because, once, many years ago, I had visited a zoo. The place was said to be the epitome of humane, caring captivity. One of my students, an ardent conservationist, had enthusiastically informed me that the animals were being saved from certain extinction.

I saw a polar bear, housed in a large enclosure, complete with ice formations and a swimming pool. He was a magnificent beast, white fur gleaming as if freshly groomed. He was obsessively walking in tight little circles.

On some Arctic tundra, he might well be in danger of a long-distance rifle wielded by a cowardly trophy-taker. Here, he was safe.

I could feel his warrior's heart dying within him.

The gorillas were not caged. They were in a large outdoor pit, surrounded by walls they could not scale, and further separated from the spectators by a metal fence. I watched, listening to mothers tell their children the animals were playing. A large male detached himself from the others, and stood facing us. Our eyes met. His said: "I am your brother. Why have you done this to me?"

I never returned to the zoo.

I did not doubt my understanding of those messages. But Target's messages had always eluded me. Perhaps my desire to believe he was attempting to communicate created what was never there.

"No magic," Lamont promised. "Just a little justice. You got no problem with justice, right, Ho?"

"I have many problems with what people *call* justice."

"Righteous," he assured me.

65

Lamont tracked through the city as if following a memorized map. We came upon a small throng, surrounding someone we could not see, but whose voice projected perfectly.

"The queen! The queen! Find the beautiful queen!" the voice invited. The accent was Mediterranean, as full of promise as those who stand outside sex establishments whispering to all those who pass that what lies inside is paradise.

Following Lamont's lead, I obtained a side view of a youngish man standing before an upturned wooden milk crate topped by a long strip of heavy cardboard. Before him he placed three playing cards, each folded in half lengthwise. He picked up the cards slowly, one at a time, and showed them to the crowd. The two of spades, the ace of clubs, and the queen of hearts.

The man gently placed the cards face-down, paused, and then began to manipulate them rapidly, switching their positions over and over.

Finished, he again asked the crowd: "Where is the queen? The beautiful queen?"

A man stepped forward and placed a ten-dollar bill over one of the cards. He turned over the card; it was the ace of clubs.

"The beautiful queen, she is hiding from you, sir," the man behind the milk carton said.

Two other people tried, unsuccessfully, before a black man in a red T-shirt with the white logo of some club on its back muscled his way through and placed a bill over the card in the middle.

"Ah! The beautiful queen reveals herself to the handsome man," the man behind the milk carton exclaimed in surprise, holding up the queen of hearts for all to see. He reached in his shirt pocket and handed several bills to the black man.

"That's the shill," Lamont whispered.

"I do not—"

"Just *watch,* Ho. You see what the card man's doing?"

"Yes," I said. "He holds the cards with his thumb so the throwing motion he makes does not dislodge the card he picked up just before."

"Like in slow motion?"

"I do not—"

"Slow motion for *you,* bro. Keep watching."

As the crowd began to thin, Lamont shoved me forward, pressing a bill into my hand. I looked down, and saw it was five dollars. I held it up.

"You want to play, Pops?" the man behind the milk carton asked.

"Please."

"Very easy. You see the beautiful queen?" he asked, holding it up in front of me.

"Yes."

"All right, now. You just watch me move her around, okay? When I stop, you put your money over her. You find her, you double your money, understand?"

"Yes," I said, again.

The man's hands flashed. As they moved, I instantly understood what Lamont had meant by slow motion.

I placed the bill over the queen.

The man gave me a cold, appraising look. Then he turned over the card.

"Pops is a winner!" he said, loudly.

I held out my hand for the money I was expecting.

"Hey, come on, Pops. You don't want to walk off a winning streak; that's bad karma, Charlie Chan. Double or nothing?"

"Very well," I said.

Again, he switched the cards, moving slightly more quickly, although no less transparently.

As he pocketed the bill Lamont had given me, I tapped the end card. It was the queen.

The card dealer took a step back. The black man in the red T-shirt started to walk toward me. I saw Lamont step into his path. Soft words were exchanged.

The card dealer watched as the black man nodded to him.

"Looks like this is not my day," the card man said. "Pops here got too much juju going. Turned my beautiful queen into a whore." He then handed me several bills. He did not return my bow.

66

"Why is this fifty dollars?" I asked Lamont, as I handed him my winnings. "It should only be twenty, is that not correct?"

"I told the monte man's partner it'd cost them half a C-note for us to get in the wind. They'll get that back in ten minutes, especially now that you pumped up all the suckers for them."

I looked back and heard the crowd demanding that the game continue.

"What if he had refused?" I asked.

"Then you would have stayed right there until he was tapped out, Ho. The shill got the message—we were selling them a license to fleece the sheep. He flashed his partner, we get paid to walk away—everybody wins."

"Everybody? They will cheat—"

"Look, Ho, any fool knows that three-card monte is all about the hands. Ain't nobody *making* those suckers play, is there?"

"No," I acknowledged.

"Beef in oyster sauce with snow-pea pods!" Lamont crowed, leading the way toward a take-out place we all knew well.

Target was clearly excited . . . and strangely silent.

67

As is our custom, Lamont and I arrived moments before the appointed time. Sometimes the area is not safe for such as Michael or Brewster, and we must guard against any incident that could endanger others. Our motives are pure. Lamont and I are not claiming territory; we are merely ensuring that it represents no danger to our brothers.

It might even be said that we are protecting others *from* our own. Years ago, before we established this procedure, Lamont and I had been so engaged in one of his schemes that we had arrived slightly late. By then, some men on motorcycles were frightening Michael and Target. They were not actually committing an assault, but their posture was menacing, and Target's shouting seemed to be spurring them on. Every time they waved the heavy chains they carried, the fear of their prey encouraged them, and they moved in closer.

"Come on, Ho!" Lamont shouted. "Those motherfuckers are gonna—"

His exhortation was interrupted by the sudden appearance of Ranger from behind what seemed to be an abandoned vehicle. The rearmost of the cyclists suddenly went to the ground. His riderless mount went forward a few feet before falling, drawing the attention of the others. Ranger let out an unearthly shriek and charged, brandishing a hooked scythe over his head.

The cyclists retreated just as Lamont and I arrived. We quickly herded Michael and Target away from the area.

Ranger came with us, walking backward so as to keep his adversaries in sight. That precaution was quite unnecessary—as soon as the unseated rider had regained his mount, they all fled, leaving only the resonation of their engines behind.

We stood together, watching.

Not watching the motorcyclists retreating; watching Ranger slowly return to a calmer stage of psychosis.

"How many did I get?" he asked Lamont, minutes later.

"I counted four," Lamont replied without hesitation.

Ranger looked across at the now-empty swath of asphalt. "Got to give it to 'em, man. Lot of outfits would've left the bodies, dead or alive. Must've been some of their top-class guys."

"They never saw you coming, bro," Lamont crooned softly.

Michael took off his overcoat and wrapped it around Ranger's shoulders—we knew Ranger would start shaking very soon, as if afflicted with ague.

Target built a fire. He can conjure flame from anywhere, but Lamont has never been able to get him to do so on request, despite pointing out the financial opportunities such "magic" would open for us.

We huddled together until Ranger's body expelled the poison that had invaded his mind.

Only then did we share our food.

68

This time, we had our feast all spread out by the time the others arrived.

As is our custom, we dined in polite silence. Although I

generally preferred the lotus position, I occasionally varied this, for fear it would come to be viewed by the others as "correct," knowing such would result in imitation.

Ranger invariably squatted, balancing his food in his lap, using his knife as a utensil. He had somehow replaced the edged weapon he had contributed toward our radio. This surprised no one.

None of the others were remotely predictable as to their dining posture. Target could use chopsticks one-handed even while pacing in circles around our perimeter, but he was always mindful never to move behind Ranger.

That afternoon, when our meal was finished, we carefully wrapped all that remained and distributed it equally. As always, Brewster refused his share, and so did Target.

Michael ceremoniously distributed the little packages of moist cloths he always carried. He was fastidious about his hands, keeping his nails trimmed and clean at all times. He had once attempted to explain to me that a man's hands are the first thing a "prospect" examines. As he was explaining the importance of this, we both seemed involuntarily drawn to look at my own hands. And I then understood that what has meaning in one world has none in another. To a stockbroker, my hands would display a life unworthy of their trust; to a martial artist, they would display a life of combat knowledge.

Once the rituals of our meal had been completed, I told our clan what Lamont and I had observed earlier.

"That building on the other side of the alley, it had fire escapes?" Michael asked. "Air-conditioning boxes in some of the windows, but not all of them?"

"Yes," I agreed, impressed at the accuracy of his guesses.

"They're warehousing it," Michael pronounced, knowingly. "The owner wants to take it co-op, but he can't get enough of the tenants to give up a rent-stabilized lease, especially with how things are now. So he's just letting the place go to hell. No maintenance, no painting, no fixing things when they break."

"He is attempting to create intolerable living conditions?" I asked.

"No," Michael dismissed my naïve speculation. "You couldn't *make* a place bad enough to get anyone to walk away from a sweet lease, not in this city. He's just cutting down on expenses. Playing a waiting game. Most of the tenants are probably pretty old. When one dies off, the owner doesn't even try to rent their unit; he starts 'rehabbing' it. Time's on his side. Between paying off some tenants to move, and others' relocating to a cemetery plot, the balance has got to tip. Soon as he gets enough people to sign on, he sells the whole thing to a co-op management outfit and walks away rich."

"This helps us how, exactly?" Lamont asked him.

"Maybe it does, a little," Michael replied, refusing Lamont's standing offer to take umbrage. "We've got to empty Brewster's library at night, so we don't want people on the other side of the alley hitting nine-one-one when they see something suspicious going on. A building like the one you described, who's going to be watching? Most of the units aren't even occupied, and the ones that are, they'll have their A/C going, blocking up the windows. Plus, when you've got a landlord who *wants* them all moving out, no way he's putting money into security cameras out back, either."

"Didn't see any," Lamont said, providing our band with

the multiple perspectives of how he and Michael would assess *any* building. "And with those fire escapes running all the way down the back, they probably got burglar bars on their other windows, too."

"No sentries?" Ranger asked, one foot in each of the two worlds he constantly moves between.

"None," I assured him.

"It's just a moving job," Michael said confidently. "And I got just the van we need."

"Where did you find—?"

"I don't mean I *got* one, Ho. I mean I found the kind we need. Like I said, the library would have everything. What we need is a Dodge Sprinter 3500, okay? That thing's got over three hundred cubic feet in the back. And it could carry all Brewster's library like it was a load of feathers."

"These are plentiful?"

"I don't know," Michael confessed. "But they look different enough from other vans that we should be able to spot one if we see it. They've got some kind of extended roof, like a big bubble on top."

"Is there any way we could obtain a photograph?"

"All we need is the coins to feed the library machine and we can print out the image," Michael said. "Nothing to it."

I looked over at Lamont, and was pleased to see he was already reaching into his pocket.

69

"You cannot sell your medication while we are completing our mission," I told Brewster later that night.

"But, Ho—"

"You sell your medication to acquire books," I said to the young man. "You know this endangers you, but still you persist. None of us has ever criticized this behavior, have we?"

"I know you don't like—"

"Man, we don't like *you* when you're not on your meds," Lamont said, bluntly. "But you *with* us, so we let it slide. That's two-way, bro. All for one, that's got a flip side. You're not in charge here. We ain't working *for* you, we working *with* you, dig it? And if you not gonna pull your weight, why the hell should the rest of us be going through all this?"

"Not to buy books!" Brewster said, his face flushed with conflicting emotions.

Ranger tensed, reacting as he often does: to tone, not content.

"We do not understand," I said to Brewster, my own tone indicating that we *wished* to understand, and were only awaiting the explanation we knew he had.

"Ho . . . Look, I was thinking. You know what would fix all this?"

"Money?" Lamont said.

"Damn right!" Brewster answered, as if Lamont's response had not been sarcasm.

"You intend to sell your medication to obtain sufficient money to hire professional movers?" I asked him. "And to rent adequate storage space?"

"I know I've got . . . problems," Brewster said. "But I'm not stupid."

"No one has ever so much as implied this," I told him,

sternly. "My question was motivated by confusion only. Do not see what is not there."

"I'm sorry, Ho. I . . . Look, here's what I figure. I can get a little money from my sister, I know I can. Plus the meds. Maybe even a hundred dollars."

"Yes?"

"Well . . . remember that time Lamont got us our radio?"

"And my compass," Ranger reminded him.

"I do," I acknowledged, cautiously.

Brewster turned to Lamont. "So . . . you could buy us a rod for a hundred dollars, couldn't you?"

"A . . . what?!?"

"You know, a . . . pistol."

"Man, that's throwing away good money. You want to kill yourself, just jump off a fucking roof."

"I don't want to kill myself," Brewster said, ignoring Lamont's anger-edged derision. "I want to pull a job."

70

Silence dropped over us as though a dictator's mandate had forbidden all speech. I do not lack patience, but I knew such a state could not be tolerated for long. Any of us, left to his own thoughts, was capable of reaching self-destructive conclusions. Our pasts all had this in common: failure to distance thought from action had resulted in tragic consequences.

I stepped into the void. "You intend to commit a robbery?" I asked Brewster, my voice devoid of judgment.

"There's no other way out," the young man said. "I got to

do what's right." He intended his voice to be that of the hardened criminals who live within the pages of his treasures, but it emerged as the cry of a frightened child.

"Might! Tight! Fight! Light!" Target clanged, returning to full volume.

Michael responded to that warning bell by reverting to his own past world: "Look, you've got a complete inventory, right?"

Brewster nodded, his lips trembling.

"People *collect* that stuff," Michael said. His voice was disparaging, but his posture excluded Brewster from whoever those "people" might be. "There's got to be price guides—you know, what they're worth and all."

Brewster retreated within himself.

"No, listen!" Michael entreated him. "I'm not saying sell them *all,* am I? Just whatever brings in the most, okay? We don't have time to get the best deal, maybe, but we can score enough to get whatever's left moved to a storage unit and pay a few months' rent in front for *sure.*"

"That's fucked up!" Ranger snarled. "Brewster *earned* those books, man. You don't see me taking my star down to some pawnshop—"

"Ranger!" I interrupted. "Please, show us your star."

"Come on, Ho. You guys have seen it a—"

"I like to look at it," Brewster said, a genuine sincerity unmistakable in his voice. "I always like to look at it."

Ranger slowly extracted a small black pouch from his waistband. Carefully he unfolded the pouch, laid it flat, and unzipped the pouch. Reaching inside, he withdrew a bronze star attached to a ribbon edged in white, with two broad stripes of red separated by a thin line of blue, also edged in white. The clasp held a five-point star with a circle at its center, on which another star was engraved.

"You see that 'V'?" Brewster said, pointing to a tiny symbol attached to the ribbon. "That stands for 'valor.' Heroism. *Combat* heroism." His voice was that of a proud son.

"Tell that to the desk soldiers at the fucking VA," Ranger said, quickly but carefully replacing his medal in its protective case and slipping it back under his khaki sweatshirt. His voice was harsh, but his face was flushed with embarrassment at Brewster's admiration.

"Your medal is well protected by that case," I said, very mildly. "I did not realize that the military issued such—"

"I'm an asshole," Ranger announced, as if answering a question about his occupation.

Target's facial muscles twitched.

Lamont folded his arms across his chest.

"Forgive me, Michael," Ranger said formally. He had learned that the American tradition of saying "I'm sorry" was a meaningless platitude, commonly uttered as vacuously as "How are you?"

"Apology" is inherently ambiguous. A man may truly regret his conduct . . . or only its outcome.

The first time Brewster had prevailed upon Ranger to display his medal in Michael's presence, it took several minutes for Ranger to produce it—he had been carrying it wrapped in rags, duct-taped to his torso.

Michael had studied the medal with great care, his eyes as calculatingly intense as a jeweler's loupe. Surprising us all, Ranger suddenly handed Michael his medal. Michael never shifted his eyes as he turned the medal over, noted its length against his own open palm, gauged its weight. He held the medal as if it were spun glass, but otherwise remained as emotionless as an assayer. When his examination was complete, he handed the medal back to Ranger. "It's beautiful" is all Michael said.

Some time later—more than days, less than a month—Michael showed us all the pouch before handing it to Ranger. No words were exchanged between them as Ranger again removed his medal and placed it inside the pouch, where it has resided since.

Michael's bow was both an acceptance of Ranger's apology and abandonment of his plan to convert Brewster's library to cash.

Thus, the burden was passed to Lamont.

71

"Pull a job?" He confronted Brewster, his voice sliding into a speech style he usually reserved for dealing with strangers. "What's your problem, boy? The government already notarized your ass. Once they start sending you those loco checks, ain't no reason to keep on *proving* you crazy."

The young man recoiled as if he had been slapped. His face burned with shame; his eyes filled with tears of humiliation.

"That whole disability deal's just a scam," Michael said hotly, putting his body between Lamont and Brewster. "I tried the same dodge myself, but I wasn't slick enough to get away with it."

"My sister's husband says I'm—"

"Fuck that faggot," Ranger sneered, glaring at Lamont. "What's he know?"

"Ho! Throw! Go! Show!"

Target's rant went unnoticed by all, as always. But some part of my spirit sensed that his use of my name was not the fortuitous rhyme it seemed. I went very still within myself, creating that pure darkness which is the ultimate invitation for light to enter.

"Everyone is right," I said.

Each man turned to look at me.

I bowed to each in turn. Then I quite deliberately lapsed into the form of speech I had once used so casually.

"To be right is not to be correct; it is to be righteous. Not all the questions have the same answer. The same words can have many meanings. The speaker is more than the speech."

"Reach! Beach! Leech! Teach!"

Again I bowed. "I apologize for my pretentiousness," I said to them all. "I wish for simplicity in all things, yet I speak as if I were some sort of prophet. I mean to say no more than this: Brewster's sister's husband is a cruel man. He is small in his soul, happiest when he inflicts pain. He calls Brewster names like 'crazy' to cause hurt. Brewster, you know this."

The young man nodded, head down.

"Has Lamont ever called you such things before today?" I asked.

Brewster shook his head.

"How often do you encounter your sister's husband?"

"Not . . . not much," Brewster said. "I stay away when I think he might be—"

"You avoid him, yes?"

The young man nodded.

"You see Lamont every day, Brewster. Do you avoid *him*?"

"Lamont?" Brewster replied, his tone implying that my question was absurd. "Lamont? Lamont's my friend."

"Why would your friend call you crazy, Brewster?"

Michael opened his mouth, then quickly snapped it shut.

"Because . . . because he wanted to talk me out of pulling a job!" Brewster said, a smile transforming his features.

"Took you long enough, fool!" Lamont said, throwing up his hands.

72

Ranger abruptly announced he was going scouting. Michael also rose to his feet. The two men moved off together.

Lamont then launched into an incredibly complex explanation of why an armed robbery could not solve Brewster's problem. The explanation was purely logistic, heavily laced with the sort of gangster jargon Brewster loves.

I sat with Target, who was calmer than I had ever seen him, never once interrupting the conversation between Lamont and Brewster. Many times, I have looked into Target's eyes, seeking knowledge. Each time, he would look away—direct eye contact disturbed him. That afternoon, he held my gaze.

Is he inviting me in? I thought to myself. *Or is he seeking to enter?*

Darkness came, making it unsafe to remain in the park.

Our questions still unanswered, we headed toward the dugout. Brewster came with us.

Michael returned just before midnight. He said Ranger was sweeping the area, and would be with us soon.

73

At first light, it was as if an old tape began to replay. Michael was trembling with the intensity that once had propelled him to such high status in the financial world, totally committed to locating the white Rolls-Royce.

"It's all lined up, Ho," he hissed, his words a forceful whisper. "Like ducks in a row. It's not about the . . . other thing. Not anymore. See, I get it now. I *really* get it. Money can't fix people, like I always thought it could. I thought if I could just get enough money then I'd be . . . whatever I wanted to be.

"But you know what? Even if money can't fix people, it can fix *things*. If we pulled off this score and we used the money to buy Brewster a safe place for his library—*buy* it, I'm saying, not stash it—that'd make it a righteous mission, wouldn't it?"

"Mission," Ranger said, as if the word itself was holy.

"If we *had* the money, it would be a righteous act to use it as you say," I told Michael. "But we do not have the money. And we cannot gamble in an attempt to obtain it."

"It's not gambling if—"

"Michael—"

"What did I tell you before, Ho? You remember?"

"Yes. A 'mortal lock.'"

"O*kay*! It can't be gambling if it's a sure thing, am I right?"

"No."

"No?"

"There is no such . . . thing as you envision, Michael. The only certainty that truly exists in all the world is uncertainty. Predicting an outcome is a skill. Some may possess it to a very high degree. But you are describing a calculation of odds, not some magical tool which never fails.

"No matter how you phrase it, we would still be gambling, Michael. That was a choice *you* made, one for which you have paid dearly. Gambling is your enemy. One you have not yet defeated." I said this gently, as I once would have done to students who had failed to master a particular technique, always expressing confidence that, one day, they *would* succeed.

"It's *not* gambling," Michael insisted. "It's only gambling when you put up an ante, when you risk something. What have *we* got to lose? I mean, say I'm wrong, okay? It still wouldn't cost us anything."

"It would cost us *time,*" I said. "That is our only currency, and we have precious little to risk. What have we to lose? Why say 'we' if you mean only yourself, my brother? Would *you* lose nothing if Brewster lost all that is meaningful to him?"

Michael deflated, shrinking before our eyes.

"Your concept is flawless, Michael," I said, addressing my words to all. "This is not about money. It *is* about a mission. A mission we undertake for our brother. By forcing us to examine ourselves, you have shown us the way."

"No draftees," Ranger said.

All turned to look at him. The weight of our silence finally compelled him to explain: "I don't mean how you get into it," Ranger went on. "I served with draftees who turned into real fighting men. But when the LT says he needs, say, four guys for a mission, you have to hold up your hand. I mean, you don't *have* to, but you're *supposed* to, see?"

"Man's telling it like it is," Lamont rasped. "No matter where you go, it's all the same. Life's nothing but a fucking war. If you can't be counted *on,* you can't be counted *in.*"

"So, Michael?" I asked.

Michael got to his feet. Then he raised his hand, volunteering for the mission.

"That's the man," Ranger said, driving a fist into his own palm.

74

"Even if for the best of causes, theft is theft," I later told Lamont. Our band had gone their separate ways, except, this time, Lamont had chosen to accompany me from the first step. Target followed along.

"I ever say it wasn't?" he countered. "All I'm saying is, if we don't come up with the coin, that boy Brewster *is* gonna get himself a gun. You know it same as I do. That look. He *needs* those books, Ho.

"Maybe the kid's no stick-up artist, but he's just like those punks you see out there every day. All *they* see is gold chains and a tricked-out Escalade, women dangling all over them like they rock stars. And you can't be in the dope game without shooters on your payroll."

"How is Brewster like those you describe?"

"He's *exactly* the same, Ho. They both sing the same song. The one every gang kid knows by heart: 'Don't Mind Dyin'.' And it don't take long to find out if they lying."

"I do not understand," I acknowledged.

"Break it down for you, then," Lamont said. "When you say you don't mind dyin', you saying you not scared of nothing, okay? You gonna *take* what you need, no matter what stands in your way. For me, when I was bopping, what you needed was 'respect,'" he said, the last word heavily laced with sarcasm bordering on disgust. "For some, that's still it. But most of these young boys today, what they want is cash. Big cash. That's what they get paid for, that rep. You know, if this guy says he's going to take someone out, he's either gonna do it or die trying, see?"

"And so for Brewster—"

"It's his books," Lamont finished for me. "But, in his head, he's hearing that same song. And I'm telling you, Ho, we don't figure out a way, that kid, he *is* gonna die trying."

"So a theft to save a life . . . ?"

"Yeah. Look, somebody *will* sell that boy a gun, and if he ever has to *shoot* it . . ."

"Boot! Loot! Hoot! Shoot!" Target clanged.

Lamont and I were struck by the same thought, as if by the same bolt of lightning. I could read on his face what was flashing in my mind. Which word would send Target off was never known in advance, but his pattern had never varied. Four words, each more or less rhyming with the original trigger, but absolutely *never* repeating the trigger word itself. And yet . . .

"Mother fucker!" Lamont said.

I understood the division into separate words of what would usually be a single vile epithet to be an expression of shock. I bowed my agreement.

We both looked at Target. Instead of the near-tranquillity into which he always lapsed after an outburst—as if a painful boil had been lanced—Target appeared disturbed, in some way. He was not agitated, nor did he appear to be bristling with tension. If anything, he looked like a man standing in the shade of a tree who could not understand why this gave him no relief from the sun.

Lamont gestured as if he was shaking dice in his right hand. He looked a question at me. I nodded.

"Some people, you put a gun in their hands, you know, sooner or later, they're going to shoot."

"Shoot! Shoot! Shoot! Shoot!" Target erupted.

I searched my mind for a related word that would evoke his clanging. "So it is the *gun,* then?" I asked Lamont.

Target did not react verbally. But his posture slumped, as if a weighty depression was imposing itself. It was then I realized that his first attempt at direct communication had drained him dry.

"Come," I said to them.

75

Target was silent throughout our walk. Lamont and I had made sure of this by not uttering a word. Target never initiates speech; he only reacts to it.

Still, before today, he had never . . .

We reached the alley behind Brewster's building. I squatted, my back to the wall but not touching it. Lamont did the same, but leaned against the brick. Target squatted as I did. I had long since noted his ability to assimilate kinetic instruction, be it the simpler positional exercises or reverse breathing. He would have made a superb martial artist, I believe. But teaching him even the most rudimentary offensive moves would have been wrong—self-control is the foundational requirement for such knowledge.

"Try again," I said to Lamont, who was unscrewing the cap of whatever bottle he held in a brown paper bag.

Lamont took a short drink, then offered the bag to me. I bowed slightly and shook my head, thus politely declining his generosity. Lamont next offered his bag to Target, who imitated my polite bow and refusal—as we knew he would.

Lamont, had he been alone with Target, would never have offered to share. Not because he was selfish, or out of a lack of respect. Lamont would not give alcohol to Target for the same reason I would not teach him techniques that might cause great injury to others.

"Man's on another planet already," Lamont had once told me. "Get some booze in his blood, who knows *what* he'd do?"

This was not a risk *any* of us would undertake.

Lamont took another drink, recapped the bottle, closed the paper bag, and nodded, as if confirming a long-held suspicion. He took a single cigarette from his coat, examined it for a moment, then lit it. After one prolonged draw, he passed it to me. I repeated my respectful declining of his offer, as did Target.

"Reminds me of being back on the yard," Lamont said, in a reflective tone. "We'd squat down, just like this, back to the wall, have a smoke, and just shoot the breeze."

Target did not react.

"Is that a prison expression, 'shoot'?" I asked.

"No, bro. It just means talking to pass the time. When you're Inside, anything you can do to kill time is good. I mean, the time is always there, right? It's not like you could actually *shoot* it or anything."

Target abandoned his correct posture to sit directly on the concrete. His head lolled forward.

"This ain't gettin' it done," Lamont said. Unnecessarily.

I reached over and took Target's hand. He accepted my grip, but did not return it. I extended my other hand to Lamont, who grasped it firmly.

"Hai!" I barked.

Target looked up and saw the three of us, linked.

"Come," I said, then drew in the deepest breath, expanding my stomach as I did so. Feeling Lamont and Target beginning to connect, I exhaled through my nose, contracting my stomach as if expelling toxins. I repeated this until I could feel the others leave on their own journeys.

Where they went, I cannot know. I went . . . searching.

76

I shifted my grip so that I could measure Target's pulse. He had reached a state of deep calmness.

I brushed a nerve juncture in his wrist. Very lightly, but enough to send an electrical signal.

With my other hand, I simply squeezed.

When Target was looking directly at me, I stood up, bringing him and Lamont along with me.

"Shoot?" I said to Target.

"Shoot! Shoot! Shoot! Shoot!"

"Show us," I half-commanded, half-pleaded, pointing to myself and Lamont.

Target blinked rapidly. His eyes seemed to change color, moving from dark blue to a much paler shade, as if the blinking were some form of rheostat.

"Shoot?" I prompted.

Target's entire body shook. His face glistened with sweat. A vein throbbed in his temple. He was a warrior in battle, against an enemy only he could see.

Slowly, he staggered forward and turned to face me, each movement clearly causing him great pain.

Target stood valiantly, his left hand over his stomach, covered by his right. Again, his body reacted to whatever shock waves were assailing him. Tendons showed in his neck. His teeth ground together.

"Shoot?" I asked, again.

Target sucked air through his nose, held it, then exhaled in the same burst. He knife-edged his right hand, then brought it up to his left eyebrow, as if saluting. He held that position, knees wobbling.

I saw it then.

"Chute?" I said to Target. "We could slide Brewster's books down a chute?"

Target fainted.

77

Lamont departed so hastily that he left his bag-wrapped bottle behind. I covered Target with my coat. Lamont quickly returned with a cardboard container of soup. As Target regained consciousness, I fed him sips of the soup until color returned to his face. With slight assistance, Target was able to sit up and finish the soup on his own.

"So, when my man sounds like he's repeating the exact word that pops his cork, he's using a homonym," Lamont said, in a hushed, awed voice.

"Homonym?"

"That's a word that *sounds* the same but has more than one meaning," Lamont explained. "You have to get that from the context. Like, if I just say the word 'pair,' you might think I was talking about two of something. But if you saw me pointing at a piece of fruit, you'd know right away what I meant. Yeah?"

"I believe so," I said, still not entirely certain. "Would an example be 'I' as in myself, and 'eye' for what I see *with*?"

"Perfect!"

"And 'whine' as in 'complain,' rather than 'wine' as in a beverage?"

"You some piece of work, old man," Lamont said, grinning broadly.

78

By late afternoon, Target was back to himself. He gave no indication that he was aware of any of the events that had transpired in his absence.

I could see that Lamont was barely able to suppress his desire to discuss the meaning of Target's communications, but he realized that it was no longer safe to assume Target could not comprehend the speech of others.

The next morning, however, before we could have any such opportunity, we came under attack from an entirely unexpected source.

"What do you call *this,* Ho?" Michael almost shouted, waving what appeared to be a large amount of money in his hand.

When I did not respond, Michael spoke so rapidly that each word was sent crashing into the one to follow. "Yesterday, I saw this race on the card at Yonkers. Aged pacing mares. I didn't need the form. I knew every single one of those girls from when they were fillies. When I saw they had Waspwaist down at thirty-to-one, I couldn't believe it! Maybe she's had trouble lately, I don't know. But when she's right, she's a total fucking monster! We only had a couple of hours to get the fourteen bucks, but we pulled it off. And *look*!"

This will never stop, I thought, despairingly. Just as Lamont was using Brewster's need for money as an excuse to return to crime, Michael had found what he would call a "loophole" allowing him to return to gambling. Michael had spread his disease by apparently convincing Ranger that they had a "mission" to obtain a certain sum of money, and I did not wish to contemplate the consequences of this deception.

Worst of all, Michael had apparently won. As Lamont had once explained to me, "A junkie gets locked up on some bullshit beef, okay? Sits maybe thirty days. Thing is, he goes in with a heavy habit, and he comes out clean. Know what happens next? He goes right out and gets himself fixed up. And *that* hit, it's like the first time all over again. Man goes in carrying a ten-bag habit—he needs that much just to keep from being sick, probably doesn't even get him a real high. But when he's clean, one bag will send him to Venus, see?"

"But why would—?"

"Because he *wants* to get to Venus, bro. 'Cause he's *been* there, and he likes it. Look at Michael. Think that fool would have ever picked up his habit if he hadn't *won*? That's what sets the hook so deep, that feeling you get when it comes. I guaran-fucking-tee you, if Michael had put down a few bets and lost every one, he never gets his nose opened. Every degenerate gambler, he's chasing that big win *again*. See, you can't miss a place unless you been there."

As Lamont's words ribboned through my mind, I literally watched suicidal depression assume human form. It stood before me, leering. My brother's mortal enemy had boldly stepped forth from its hiding place within him, bristling with confidence.

My reaction was not strategic but reflexive. "Why did you need fourteen dollars?" I asked Michael, giving myself a few precious seconds to study my opponent before we did battle.

"I *had* the winner, Ho. But what good is that if I can't capitalize? So I needed to wheel her on top in the exacta."

My blank-faced expression was not to buy time—Michael had switched to a language foreign to me. He noticed this at once, and realized an explanation was required: "An exacta, it's just what it sounds like, Ho. You have to get the horse that comes in first *and* the one that comes in second, *exactly* in that order, okay? There's eight horses going. So with seven bets, we *guarantee* that, if our horse wins, we cash, no matter which of the rest comes in second."

"Ah."

"Naturally, the goddamned chalk comes second," Michael said, as if he had been cheated out of something rightfully his. "But we still cashed good. Five hundred and seventy-one dollars and forty cents, Ho."

"It is not nearly—"

"That's my point! But now, with this kind of stake, I can parlay it into—"

"Michael . . ." I said. My voice trailed off into helplessness, as I realized I was no match for the opponent sneering at me from within my friend.

Lamont immediately stepped into the fray. "That is totally fucked, bro!" Catching Ranger's eye, Lamont drew him into the fight: "That's not the mission, man. That's just your jones kicking in."

"No!" Michael said, angrily. "I mean, we *need* money to move Brewster's library, am I right?"

"Sure you are," Lamont answered, still looking at Ranger. "And what you scored is exactly what we need for *supplies*. We need *gear* to pull this off, and you just won us enough to—"

"Restock!" Ranger cut him off.

"But I'm the one who won the money," Michael protested.

Finally seeing an opening, I struck. "It was Ranger who *obtained* the money you used *to* win, is that not so?"

Under Ranger's unforgiving glare, Michael's only response was "If you put it like that, Ho."

"And Ranger did so because you assured him that it was in furtherance of the mission?" I persisted, delicately poised between needing to impress the consequences of Michael's flirtation with disaster on him and not igniting Ranger.

Many times, during moments of coherency, Ranger would tell us that the worst thing about being a soldier was "They lied to us." Whether his accounts—"fragging" a platoon leader who had ordered what the troops believed would be walking into their certain deaths; "taking out" a comrade-in-arms whose cowardice under fire had endangered them all—were accurate, I could not determine. But I *had* been present at other times, and I could well envision how Ranger would process the information that Michael had—to be blunt—used him to obtain gambling money.

"It *was* for the mission," Michael protested. "And I came through, didn't I?"

"Let us look together," I said, beckoning my brothers to stand with me on the knife-point balance of our kinship. "If you saw a *single* opportunity, a unique opportunity, to enable us to stock up on the provisions we will need to complete *our* mission, you did, in all truth, come through, Michael. Just as you said.

"But, surely, you would not expect any of us to view gambling as a way to accumulate funds? Who knows the folly of such reasoning better than you? It is from you that we all learned such a vital truth. That is why such conduct is banned among us."

"Banned! Scanned! Can! Band!" Target erupted.

"Sonofabitch," Lamont muttered softly. "You get it, Ho?"

"Hai," I replied. I turned to Michael. He looked around the circle. I cannot know what he saw. I could only hope he saw what I did: his family.

"Sure!" he finally said. "That bet, it was like an . . . exception, right? Ranger always says, when you're in the field, you have to improvise. The only thing that matters is the mission, not how you get it done."

With that, Michael ceremoniously handed the money to Lamont, being careful to include the coins. Ranger had regarded Lamont as our "quartermaster" ever since Lamont had presented him with the compass he now used to navigate about the city, so the gesture was doubly meaningful.

"Do you understand what Target just told you, Michael?" I asked him.

"Target?" he said, confused. As with all of us—until very recently—he regarded Target's verbal explosions as devoid of actual meaning. He would no more attempt to understand Target's speech than he would the sounds pigeons make as they descend upon a discarded piece of bread.

"Target is saying you *can* do it, Michael. He has expressed the confidence we *all* feel in you. He understands that what you did was not a moment of weakness, or a breaking of your vow—it was your way of contributing to the mission."

Michael's eyes showed he understood what was being offered to him—another chance to be one of us.

"I got it, Ho," he said. "And thanks for the vote, Target."

Target looked at him blankly.

Lamont patted his outer pocket, where he had placed

Michael's gambling winnings. "This'll buy us some very fine tools for the work we gotta do."

"Lamont—" I began.

"Just thinking out loud," Lamont cut me off, holding up both hands, palms facing me.

"Mission-specific," Ranger said.

"What about hiring a PI?" Brewster suddenly intervened.

"A what?" Lamont said, just short of annoyed.

"A private investigator, I mean," Brewster told him. "You know, someone who can go through records, track people down, stuff like that."

"And who the fuck do *we* want to track down?" Lamont asked, clearly out of patience with Brewster's fantasies.

"The white Rolls-Royce," Brewster said, as if stating the obvious.

"Jesus H.—"

"That, too, would be a gamble," I interrupted, much as I would deflect a strike . . . not blocking, redirecting. "I do not know the hourly rate charged by such people, but it seems unlikely we could purchase enough time to complete such a complex investigation."

"It's even worse than a gamble," Michael said.

We all froze, each of us in his own way. For Michael to reject the idea of risking money on what he had previously considered a "mortal lock" was impossible to absorb.

"Look," Michael went on, as if unaware of the shock wave he had sent through us all, "what's to stop this PI guy from taking *our* info and using it himself?"

"They have a code of ethics," Brewster protested.

"So do stockbrokers," Michael said. "And lawyers."

At that, Lamont extended his fist for Michael to tap.

"Michael's right," Ranger added. "That white Rolls is ours. It's on the books. Our next mission, right after this one. No outsiders allowed."

"One! Run! Done! Son!" from Target.

We were a family once again.

79

Brewster was the first to leave that morning, but not before renewing his promise not to sell his medications. I knew he would be trying again to convince his sister to allow him to store his library in her house. I knew he would be refused. Brewster knew this as well, but he would not be able to *accept* it in an unmedicated state—the stress would cut him loose from his tenuous mooring, and he would be lost to us all.

Ranger and Michael departed together, their plans unknown.

Target chose to accompany Lamont and myself.

We still had some money remaining from Lamont's manipulation of the card-cheating team, so no fishing was required in order for us to eat.

I felt no pity for the cheaters. Only among humans is there no natural food chain, with pre-designated predators and prey. Those of our species who become predators do so by choice. When they themselves become prey, this is simply a return to the natural order of things.

"It's not what you do, brother. It's what you do it *for,* and who you do it *to*—that's what makes it right or wrong."

Instantly, I recognized that the narcissism I had been struggling to destroy for so many years had retained its presence, burying itself deeper and deeper as my self-scrutiny increased. I had chopped down the tree, but left its taproot untouched. Yes, I no longer pontificated before adoring audiences, but I still occasionally uttered my pronouncements to myself.

Is not a narcissist always his own most appreciative audience? I thought, filled with self-disgust at the revelation.

I pride myself that I can read the body of an individual the way another could read a book. I do not "sense" the attack of an opponent; I *see* it, as if already in motion. In contrast, I believe my own body to be unreadable. My face betrays nothing; my eyes are reflectors, not windows. And my body is always at rest within itself. But Lamont had read the supposedly unreadable, stepping into my internal train of thought as if it had been a conversation between us.

"I do not understand," I lied, as I would conceal an injury from an opponent.

"Remember when Brewster said it was all coming down? Maybe it takes that, sometimes. 'Cause, the way I see it, it's all coming *together,*" Lamont said. "Just check it out, Ho. We know what's gotta get done, right? Target showed us how we can get the books out, but we still need cash to move them, never mind find a place to take them to, okay? Michael always wants to roll the dice, but it's not his own money he'd be playing with . . . and the crazy bastard finally *got* that."

At a look from me, Lamont paused, then said, "I don't mean he's got the money, Ho. I mean, he's got it *down.* He understands he can't be gambling with money we need to save Brewster's library. Not because he's scared to, because he don't even *want* to. Not anymore, anyway.

"And Ranger, he's up for any damn thing, but you can't be turning a pit bull loose at a carnival—he might start looting popcorn, or he might figure people make for a better snack. It *is* coming down. Down to *us,* brother."

"I will not—"

"Yeah, you will," Lamont interrupted. "You already did, plenty of times. What's the difference between straight-up stealing, and betting against a man you know doesn't have a chance to win?"

"Such people choose their own—"

"Yeah. That's right. All we did was go Robin Hood on their ass."

"By their own conduct, they *invited*—"

"And a dope dealer *doesn't*?"

I had no answer for that.

80

"I haven't hot-wired a car since I was a kid," Lamont said, as we walked toward Brewster's building. "The way they do it today, it's either some sad-ass amateur—you know, pop the circle out of the steering column with a dent-puller, stick in a screwdriver, and hope for the best—or a pro specialist with his own set of code-breakers. The amateur, he wants to go joyriding. The pro, he's just filling an order."

"You are speaking of the van?"

"Yeah. Brewster goes up to his library. We figure out a

way to make some kind of chute, slide everything down to the van. Between you, me, and Target, we can load it up in a few minutes."

"Target?"

"The man can do anything you can do, Ho. Well, maybe not *anything*. Not the, you know, voodoo stuff. But . . . hey, show the man, bro!"

I did not react.

Then I realized Lamont was speaking to Target. Directly to him.

But Target would not meet Lamont's eyes. He focused only on mine.

Motioning with a slight movement of my head, I guided us onto a new path.

81

Luzanne was once one of us. Even though she earned sufficient money to afford a place of her own, she would often spend weeks at a time with our band.

"This is where I can be me," she said, one night.

"Because of . . . ?" Lamont said, tapping his Adam's apple to signal Luzanne that he understood she was a male.

"No. There's plenty of he-shes working the Meat Market," Luzanne dismissed Lamont's too-simple explanation. "That's like being a cancer patient on a ward. Some are worse than others, but everything's always about the *cancer*. That's all they talk about, all they think about.

"You can't have friends. I mean, you're all 'Girlfriend!' on the street, but you're *working* that street. That *same* street. Even when you take a little break, have a smoke, get the . . . taste out of your mouth, what do you talk about? Which john ripped off which girl. Which cop is working shakedown patrol. How much you made last night. Lies about how your rich boyfriend's going to take you away from all this soon. Schemes and dreams, that's all there ever is.

"But here, with you all, I'm just me. Luzanne. Not Luzanne the freak magnet. Not Luzanne the fake name on my mailbox. When I met Ho, I could see he knew it *all.* I don't mean like you did," she said to Lamont, "I mean *everything*. So, when he said to come with him, I did."

"Yet you left," I had reminded her.

"I'll come back for good someday, Ho. You know, I always wondered about 'Homeless.' That word, it can't be like this huge umbrella over every one of . . . you. Just like there can't be one over all of us, either. Trannies who car-trick, I mean. Some of us, maybe we didn't have any other choice. Or maybe the other choices were worse. The real young ones, it's like they don't even know there *are* other choices. There's even some who . . . I don't know how to put it, but I know they don't have to be out there. Like they had a whole menu, and picked out the dish they really wanted."

"Hai."

"That's what I learned, Ho. I want a life that's my choice, too. I'm not ready. Not yet. So I come and be with you for a while, then I go back to . . . what I do. But you notice how I stay longer each time I come? One day, I'll be back for good."

"You will always be welcome," I promised her.

82

As we entered the Park, Luzanne entered my thoughts. In daytime, the Park is always full of exhibitionists, allegedly "working out." I was originally puzzled by this, until Luzanne called it "voguing," and explained the meaning of that term.

She would have been the first to help with a solution to relocating Brewster's library. I am sure of this.

But Luzanne has been gone for years. Returning from her work late one night, she had been beaten to death by a gang of thugs on a subway platform. The killers were apprehended almost immediately. They admitted what they had done, but claimed Luzanne had attempted something so obscene—it does not bear repeating—that they went into a rage. The court must have accepted their explanation in some way—they are all free today.

I had learned this only because an old newspaper I had intended to use as padding displayed a headline about the outrage of certain groups over the lenient sentences handed down to Luzanne's murderers.

Thoughts of Luzanne had flooded my mind, as if propelled by the blazing sunlight. Her light reminded me of Chica's.

And of my vows.

83

With so many seeking to draw attention to themselves, there was no difficulty locating a place from which we would be unobserved. Always there is this parallelism between our world and theirs: we seek what others discard; we use what others find useless; and their lack of interest is our camouflage.

That day, in the sunlight-defying gloom of dying trees, I executed a "high forms" kata. Though originally intended as a method of practicing and perfecting various techniques, kata has become its own form of competitive sport. Today, it is the sole method by which "promotion" is earned in some styles. In my former life, I might have expounded at great length about this perversion of purity. One of my favorite pearls of recycled wisdom was to compare kata to ballet—not in a disparaging manner, as a lesser "master" might, but to demonstrate how the acme of each art required great skill, and was entitled to respect. Left unsaid was the message that neither art had developed as a defense against violence.

I performed the forms as if underwater. Each movement correct, but radically slower than would be acceptable to judges.

Target watched. Target always watches. I could not discern any unusual alertness in his posture, or any change of expression.

Lamont watched as well. He was not watching me; he was on guard. Lamont believes this city's streets are fields of gazelles, watched by lions. Any gazelle that appeared too crippled to outrun the lions would quickly become their target.

I had learned many things from Lamont over the years, but this lesson had been taught to me before Lamont had been born. Some might reason that The Homeless would enjoy a kind of immunity, because preying on obviously impoverished individuals would be profitless. But the war had taught me well. Vulnerability is the sadist's ultimate aphrodisiac. My first night on that park bench had merely confirmed what I have known ever since an evil sergeant had ordered a young boy to accompany him to his final resting place.

I had not performed a true kata for many years, yet I was unsurprised at the fluidity of my movements. The body retains muscle memory long after the limbs and joints and tendons have lost their ability to execute what the mind commands. Age has not altered my lifelong habits of self-maintenance, and years of living without a home had provided endless opportunities for me to maintain the flexibility needed for survival.

Three times I performed the micro-motioned kata.

Then I turned to Target, bowed, and said, "Now it is your turn."

"Turn! Churn! Burn! Learn!" he clanged.

I stood, unmoved.

Lamont lit a cigarette.

All around us, people enjoyed their lives. At a distance.

Just as Lamont was grinding out the stub of his cigarette in disgust, Target stepped into the exact spot I had vacated.

He breathed deeply several times. Then he imitated my kata to such a stunningly correct degree that I was shocked. Certainly, kata is initially taught in slow motion. But mine had been no beginner's kata; it would have been for advanced students only. Yet, by his third repetition, the difference between Target's movements and mine would require an expert's eye to discern.

I bowed to Target. More deeply this time. He *returned* the bow—the first time he had ever done so.

Gray butterflies of fear hovered over the happiness in my heart. Had I erred yet again? In my desire to teach Target certain techniques which would enable him to assist us in loading a van with Brewster's books, had I awakened a dragon?

Because, through teaching, I had learned: Target was an idiot savant of violence.

That knowledge taught me that true humility could never be mine until I progressed beyond my standard refusals of the mantle of leadership the others always sought to place upon me. In speech, respect and condescension are too closely allied. Only conduct conveys truth.

"How do you want to do it?" I asked Lamont.

84

"Dope dealers, they *sound* perfect. But you look close, they're strictly a no-go," Lamont told us all that night.

"Tactical?" Ranger asked, as tranquilly as a stick of dynamite with an unlit fuse. In his vernacular, it was not "on" yet.

"Kind of," Lamont said. "The big dope-men, they *got* money. And they ain't about to report getting it ripped off, either. But that kind, they never walk alone. No way we could jack one of them. Even if we pulled it off, there'd still be witnesses. And a whole *bunch* of gunslingers looking to collect the bounty on us, too."

Lamont looked around the circle, as if expecting some opposition, especially from Ranger. I could feel the others look toward me, but I kept my entire focus on Lamont, encouraging by example.

Lamont lit a cigarette. Then he said, "The street-level guys, they might be carrying some cash, might not. The only ones *we'd* be able to get to would be holding a few bags, max. You want any more than that, they just steer you to the spot. That means a steel door with a slot, and a couple of shooters behind it, blast anything coming through."

"What about the roof?" Ranger asked, still without any sign of his psychosis emerging.

"That could work," Lamont said, perhaps instinctively realizing that a side argument over military tactics would be an error in judgment. "But they'd still get too much advance warning—more than enough to make what we need disappear into a safe or whatever. Remember, all we want is cash, not product."

I reluctantly admitted the twinge of jealousy I experienced as I observed how skillfully Lamont had acknowledged the value of Ranger's input while not allowing it to distract the others.

"Not many people carry real cash," Michael said. "Even the most legit citizen probably doesn't walk around with a couple of grand in his pocket. It's all plastic now."

"Professional gamblers?" Brewster said.

When he got no response, he took it for a lack of understanding, and gave us all a short course on mythical men who worked some kind of "circuit." Pool hustlers, card players, dice men . . . all traveling about the country, their pockets stuffed with money so they could "stake" themselves into "the big game" in whatever town they came upon.

"Take too long to find one," Lamont skillfully dismissed the idea. I noted how he had finessed what another might have rejected as patently insane, thus achieving his objective without causing hurt. "Besides, like Michael says, they all work off plastic these days. You *really* want to try rolling dice, hit some guy withdrawing from an ATM at night. Chances are, you get a hundred bucks . . . and ten years Upstate."

"There are still areas where all transactions are in cash, are there not?" I asked deferentially, thinking of my poor lost Luzanne.

"That closes the circle!" Michael half-shouted, leaping to his feet. "Listen," he said, sitting down immediately and moderating his voice, as though he understood how close he had come to the edge, "you know where you can always find an ATM? In a strip club. And they have to keep those things *loaded,* you see where I'm going?"

"Hit a *strip* club?" Lamont said, his voice a perfect blend of sarcasm and sneer. Why he saw no need to mollify Michael as he had Ranger and Brewster was not apparent to me.

"No! For Chrissakes, just *listen,* okay? I'm saying, we're talking street-level, right? So who *always* gets paid in cash besides dope dealers? Hookers, am I right?"

"We're not—" Ranger began, but Michael cut him off.

"Of *course* not hookers!" he said, indignantly. "How much cash could any of them be carrying at one time, anyway? But what do you think they do with that money, put it in their checking account?"

"They hand it over—" Lamont began.

"To their *pimps,*" Michael finished for him. "There's two

kinds of pimps: the executive types who run the out-call services, and the old-style guys like in the movies—you know the kind I mean."

"Black?" Lamont said, again without acknowledging the value of whatever Michael might be saying.

"Damn right," Michael shot back. "That's how it is—money players go where they're allowed to play, am I right? Look at the NBA. There's guys on the court bringing in mega-bucks, but they don't own the teams, do they? So, when you see pimps driving flashy cars, sporting all that jewelry, you know *their* girls are walking the street. That means their pimps have got to be out there, too. Keep their eyes on the merchandise, make sure they're *working*. Probably picking up the cash, too."

"It's true," Lamont said, quietly. "I remember back in the day—"

"This is *today,* man! And it's still going on, only a little more on the down-low, since the IRS started paying attention. The kind of pimp *we're* looking for, he's not into mutual funds or CDs, trust me. His business, it's strictly cash-and-carry. He's always got to be ready if any of his girls get pinched. If the cop lets them make a call, you know what *he* needs. Any lawyer he calls that hour of the night is going to want to see green before he stands up at the arraignment."

"Part of the game," Lamont acknowledged, a trace of surprised respect in his voice. "Got to have a flash roll, too."

"And we don't want one who drives last year's Caddy, am I right?" Michael said, in his deal-closer's voice. "The one we want, *his* dream car would be a white Rolls-Royce!"

85

"This is perfect," Lamont assured me, later. "Michael's off on his damn Moby-Dick thing, so he's out of our way. And the best part is, he's got Ranger going with him. Brewster can't play—the boy's never been blooded."

None of us are unchained. I did not "think" this; it was no epiphany. It was not an example of the "insights" I once considered it my duty to share with others, the toxic harvest of the wisdom I had acquired as I descended to "master." No, this was as if I had just been attacked by a force against which I was powerless. A force of such speed and skill that it could strike and retreat in the same motion.

"Please" is all I said to Lamont.

I sat on the sidewalk, close by a subway grille. Lamont and Target fished on each side of me.

I closed my eyes.

Honesty in all things. Had I truly been so? Had I kept my vow? Achieved my goal? My internal pontifications were proof that I had not. But this was not the source of my pain. I hurt because the truth had come to me: in renouncing all worldly possessions, I finally saw the selfishness inherent in that very act.

Had I merely kept the money I had possessed at the time—not spent it, but stored it somewhere—I might have come to understand that what I had so dramatically rejected as meaningless was merely an extension of the "wisdom" I had been imposing on others. Yes, it had been "my" money. Mine to do with as I wished. But had I been focused on anything but my*self,* I would have realized that, someday, it might be meaningful to my brothers.

Even a tiny fraction of what I had tossed away would have saved Brewster's library. Saved his life.

Instead, we were now reduced to desperate measures to achieve the same end. Honor-bound to protect Brewster's library, Lamont and I were equally bound not to bring harm to any of the others.

Others? Yes, I answered the contemptuous tone of my spiritual questioner. Ranger, Michael, and Brewster are all fragile, each in his own way. Target cannot even function at a minimal level without attachment to others. Only Lamont and I could survive the incarceration we must risk to obtain the necessary money.

You are their protectors? We are all protectors of one another, but each in his own way, I answered the implied accusation. Lamont and I are simply the only ones capable of *this* particular task. We are not superior to the others; we have superior skills in some areas, just as they do.

Remember, I admonished my spirit, this plan was not mine, it was Lamont's.

Lamont longs for his life.

Thus was the circle of truth revealed to me. Lamont would always be a poet—that was in his soul. But he would not wish to return to that experience. When he speaks with pride about his past, it is always to highlight the difference between the street warriors of a generation ago and the gun-crazed children who call themselves "gangs" today.

Had Lamont worked so hard to convince me that

crime was our only hope so he could be a gang leader once again?

Are the only truly honest people on this earth those others regard as insane?

Once, I might have pondered such a question, telling myself I was seeking the Tao.

Today, my search is for money.

86

Lamont and Target had been surprisingly successful in the time I was gone—apparently several hours, given the shifting of the shadows on surrounding buildings. We could have ourselves a fine supper once more.

We approached Kabuki, a most superior Japanese restaurant I had been visiting for many years . . . always via its back door. The proprietor, who felt he "knew" me, had given orders with kitchen staff that I should be allowed to purchase whatever "extra" they had available for whatever money I had on hand.

The proprietor and I had never met in my former life. His knowledge of me was part of whatever mythology surrounded my reasons for walking away from that life, a mythology doubtless developed by former students who were left with the task of explaining the closing of the dojo and the departure of their sensei.

My fluency in Japanese coupled with my humble demeanor probably only enhanced whatever myth the proprietor had chosen to believe. So he honored my unspoken wish that I not be questioned concerning my reasons for living as I did. I, in turn, honored his generosity by never requesting more food than whatever sum of money I had to offer would reasonably purchase on any given occasion.

Occasionally, one of the workers would surreptitiously enhance the order. I did not know which one was responsible, or if this was some group decision. But since none sought recognition, I could not disrespect the gesture by refusing—as I would have in my former life.

What I did notice was that this enhancement of my food orders did not depend on any single individual, because the kitchen staff was always changing.

Thus, I assumed the proprietor himself had given the instructions.

A man can be humble without lowering himself. A humble man may accept a gift, but must never embarrass those who give anonymously by expressing his gratitude directly.

As we approached the back door that evening, we noticed two Chinese youths exiting. They were dressed alike, in elaborately embroidered silk jackets. They passed by us without reaction of any kind.

"Shadow Riders," Lamont said, just as we heard the distinctive sound of motorbikes bursting into life.

"What are Shadow Riders?" I asked him.

"Gang boys. You can tell from the jackets. They got their name because they all ride. Not hogs, like the Ching-a-Lings up in the Bronx, little scooters, like you see in those kung-fu movies."

I was deeply puzzled. The back door of the restaurant was not open to the public. Intruders at the front would be met with force. So those gang members must have been invited. But for a Japanese restaurant to invite *Chinese* visitors?

Nevertheless, I knocked politely. Two palm-thuds, then a single knuckle-rap. My personal signal.

The door opened. As the staff bustled about filling my order—it would be a very large one, for I had brought twenty dollars, far more than usual—a palpable odor of fear overpowered even the aromatic cooking in progress.

Selecting a cook I knew had been there for years, I asked if I might impose upon him to request a brief audience for me with the proprietor.

The cook bowed more deeply than my apparent station in life should have warranted. He left without a word, returned almost immediately, and silently pointed toward a side door.

As I opened that door, I found myself in a lushly carpeted corridor. At the end of the corridor, I could see the proprietor through the open door of what was clearly his private office.

He stood up as I entered, and greeted me as if I were an invited guest, worthy of respect. I bowed my thanks. At his invitation, I sat on the floor beside a small, ornately carved table. He took his place across from me. How he signaled I do not know, but a young woman entered, and performed the formal tea ceremony with all the elegance of a true geisha before she departed wordlessly.

"May I be permitted to ask a question?" I said.

"Of course," he replied, as if no other response could have entered his mind.

"Shadow Riders?"

"Ah! You must have seen them leave, the filthy little parasites."

"They are beggars?"

"They are thugs," the proprietor said. "They fancy themselves as Yakuza would in our country, but they are only children. They lack honor. For skill with a sword, they substitute firearms."

"Why would such be allowed—?"

"It is a tax," the proprietor said. "Not a government levy, but a cost of doing business all the same. If they are not paid, weekly, they will cause great damage. Other establishments which refused payment suffered in many ways, from staged disturbances that frightened customers to, in one known case, actual arson. They 'protect' my business from such possibilities. Insurance only compensates one for damage; they prevent damage from occurring."

"By not committing it."

"Hai!" he said, shrugging his shoulders to indicate he accepted this to be an inevitability. "Were it not them, it would be others," he said, confirming my interpretation of his gesture.

"I humbly thank you for granting me an audience," I said.

07

On my way out, I picked up the huge sacks of food the kitchen had prepared. I handed one to Lamont and another to Target, and we headed crosstown to our dugout to share our bounty.

"They're trying to tell me things," Brewster said abruptly. "I ask them to stop, but they never do."

"How much did you get paid?" Michael said, angrily.

"I—"

"You little pussy," Ranger said. His voice was chilling. "You are *not* going to fuck up the mission, you understand?"

"I was trying to help—"

"No freelancers," Ranger chopped off Brewster's feeble words with the machete of his icy rage.

However it had occurred, he and Michael viewed Brewster's selling his medication as something even graver than a personal affront. Neither focused on the fact that the mission was on Brewster's behalf. Or on the danger Brewster put himself in whenever he went off his medication for too long. They saw Brewster's act for what it was: a threat to the unifying force that protected us all.

"I don't like the meds anyway," Brewster said, more aggressively than he had ever spoken before. "I hate them. You know . . . all that spastic stuff they make me do. I don't even think I need them, not really."

"You don't hear the voices when you're taking them," Lamont said. Nonjudgmental, merely stating a truth we all knew.

"They're not that bad," Brewster said, the aggression gone from his voice.

"We had a guy in our outfit," Ranger said, his voice still without warmth. "Rocco. Man loved his weed. Toked through it like it was a pack of Lucky Strikes. Had his way, he would've *stayed* wherever that stuff took him, okay? He'd light up anywhere."

"But if he was on a mission—" Michael said, sagely, as if he was about to join Ranger's effort to educate Brewster.

"Mission? Fuck. I saw Rocco light up in the middle of a

firefight one time! Puffing away and blazing away at the same time. Thing is, that was Rocco. And you know what Rocco was? A guy who had your back. A guy who grabbed the point when it was his turn. He didn't get high to work up his nerve; he did it for the same reason a lot of guys did. You're out there, a million miles from home, trying to kill a bunch of people who live there. And they're trying to kill you. After a while, everyone—everyone on the fucking *ground,* I mean—gets the point."

Ranger lapsed into silence.

"Which was . . . ?" Michael asked.

"Yeah," Ranger answered. "What *was* the fucking point?" The depth of sadness in his voice was so profound that to call it "depression" would be to call a bone marrow infection a flesh wound.

"Brewster," I said. "I cannot speak for anyone but myself. And for myself I say this: if you do not return to your medication, I will not participate in the mission to save your library."

"You can deal me out, too, bro," Lamont told him.

"Bro! Know! Grow! Show!" Target clanged.

"Would you go with me, Ho?"

"Where do you want to go, Brewster?"

"To see my therapist. Levi."

"Why would you want me to do this?" I asked, wondering if Brewster was hallucinating. Why would he be on a first-name basis with a therapist?

"Levi says I have to stay on my meds, too. So I can get my check. It's the same place Ranger goes, but they don't make *him* take meds. If you went with me, maybe Levi would tell me why."

"Has he not told you?"

"Yeah. But . . . but you're different, Ho. He'd talk to you different, too. I know he would."

"When do you next see your therapist?"

"I can go anytime I want."

This, too, sounded bizarre to me. I imagined one would require an appointment. And again wondered if Brewster had slipped forever into a world of his own creation. But I had no choice. My debt was not to Brewster; it was to our . . . unit.

"I will go with you tomorrow morning," I said. "But only if you give your word that you will not go off your medications again."

"If you believe Levi, I'll believe you, Ho."

"That is deliberately evasive," I said, bluntly. "I am not going to bargain with you. I will not substitute my judgment for that of a trained professional. This cannot be decided by what I believe. Or even what you believe, Brewster. Either you must make the commitment, on your honor, or you will undertake the mission without me." I paused, and looked around the circle. "Lamont and Target have already spoken as well."

"Your number's been called, kid," Ranger told him. "You either stand up with us, or go sit someplace else."

"I gave back my winnings," Michael told him, conveniently overlooking how he had come by them.

"Ho?" Brewster pleaded.

"I said I would go with you tomorrow, Brewster. And I will. That is what a man of honor does. He keeps his word. We are, all of us, damaged in some way. But a man whose word is worthless is a worthless man."

"Now! Now! Now! Now!" Target shouted. No interpretation was required.

"I swear I won't ever go off my meds again," Brewster said. The young man broke into sobs.

Lamont passed around paper plates from our stack as if he were dealing from a deck of cards, concentrating on his task.

"What is an ACT Team?" I asked, as Brewster and I entered a storefront with "Community Outreach Service Center" neatly lettered on its blacked-out front glass.

"That's where Levi is," he said, as if he had just provided a detailed explanation.

The receptionist was a shapely mixed-race woman whose appearance was clearly of great importance to her. She favored Brewster with a dazzling smile. When she picked up her telephone without asking Brewster's name, I assumed he was a well-known client.

I made for the chairs on the far wall, expecting a long wait, but Brewster tugged at my coat sleeve, silently bidding me to stay where we were.

Almost immediately thereafter, a powerfully built black man with a shaved head came over to us. He looked like those who are placed on guard outside exclusive clubs, but instead of a menacing scowl, he presented a cheerful, welcoming countenance. "Brewster. My *man*! Come on. Levi's wrapping up something; he'll be with you in a few."

As I began to follow Brewster, the large man turned and

blocked my path, his tone and posture transforming him from Brewster's friend to his guardian. "Something you want?"

"I am with Brewster."

"This is Ho, Earl," Brewster said. "I asked him to come with me today."

The black man immediately offered his hand. I took it, noting his grip was intended to convey a comforting strength, not a demonstration of power.

We passed a young Latina with large, luminous eyes. She smiled at Brewster, exchanged what was meant to be a covert look with Earl. "Welcome," she said to me. I bowed, hiding my surprise. I always fancied myself as a man not given to assumptions, but recognizing my own surprise at being greeted formally was proof that my self-assessment had been inflated.

Brewster seemed to take great pride in his intimacy with those we encountered. "Hi, Joanne!" he called out to a blond, blue-eyed woman, who responded with "Good to see you, Brewster."

A smallish woman walked over to us, her movements supple and self-assured. "Who's this?" she asked Earl.

"Name's Ho," Earl replied. "He's with Brewster, Glo."

When that response appeared to satisfy her, Brewster took this as affirmation of his own status. I could feel his presence expand with the assurance that he was *known,* a person, not a "case." I understood that the exchange between Gloria and Earl was a technique of some sort, but a technique beyond my experience.

I was introduced to Hiram, a pensive young man who wore his hair in two thick braids, as if to emphasize his Native

American heritage. He was far more formal in his greeting, as if to tell me that his heritage was no mere costume—I was, after all, quite obviously his elder.

Next I met Wendy, who looked like some of the women I had seen at a poetry reading Lamont had taken me to at the public library the year before.

"That was Adanna," Brewster told me as an African woman in a tan sweater flew past, obviously too busy to exchange even a word.

"And that's Dr. B.," he confided, as we passed the office of a red-haired woman so deep in reviewing papers on her desk that she did not look up as we walked by.

The noise level varied from room to room, from silence to shouting.

"Open for business," Earl said, indicating an open door. He rapped on the jamb, and called out, "Brewster's here to see you, boss. And he brought a friend, too."

The man who must be Levi stood up. He was moderately tall, well muscled, with close-cropped blond hair and the high cheekbones and blue eyes I associate with Slavic antecedents, wearing an unbuttoned denim shirt over a thin black jersey.

He offered his hand. I responded, wondering if there was some special grip all those of his profession had to learn—his was precisely the same as Earl's had been.

Brewster sat down without being invited. I thought this impolite, but accepted that I was a guest of another culture, and must be respectful of its rules.

"When did you go off your meds?" Levi immediately asked, in a conversational tone which implied that Brewster had already disclosed his lapse—that such was a fact, not a topic for discussion.

"Five days ago," Brewster replied. "And I feel okay."

"Uh-huh. Is that why you brought a friend with you today?"

"No, Levi. This is Ho. He . . . he understands things. I thought you would, like, explain to him how come I have to take the meds. Then he could, you know, explain it to me."

"Like an interpreter, huh?"

"Yeah!" Brewster said, with genuine enthusiasm.

"Brewster," Levi said, without inflection of any kind, "you know all about confidentiality. You know I can't discuss your case with anyone unless you give permission."

"But that's why I brought him. I mean, *I* brought Ho. Isn't that the same as giving permission?"

"Sure," Levi agreed. As he spoke, I heard a distinct whistling sound through his nose—it had been broken at least once. This did not fit my imagined picture of "therapist." Nor did his style of dress, and the way he spoke to Brewster more like a friend than a patient. "But *you* know Mr. Ho, Brewster. I don't. So I have to ask him to sign a paper that says anything he hears in this room can't be repeated. Okay?"

Not knowing to whom Levi had addressed his question, I said, "I will sign your paper."

I stared at the page long enough to allow my other senses to explore the immediate environment, then deliberately scrawled some undecipherable "signature" at the bottom.

"How do you want to do this?" Levi asked Brewster.

"Couldn't you just, like, tell him?"

Levi turned slightly to connect his eyes with mine. "Brewster is schizophrenic," he said, using the word as though he were saying Brewster had brown hair—a description, not a judgment. "He hears voices. The voices aren't his friends. They try to make Brewster do things he doesn't want to do. Sometimes, they succeed. That's when Brewster ends up arrested, and we have to go and get him. That's how Brewster came to us in the first place: a referral from Rikers."

I knew Rikers was a jail or prison of some kind. But I had also thought Brewster had never been arrested. So all I said was "Yes?"

"Schizophrenia is incurable. But it *is* manageable, with the right combination of medication and therapy. It's our job to make sure Brewster gets both."

"Brewster says he does not need this medication."

Levi studied my face for a moment. "But you already know that's not true," he said.

"Yes," I admitted, noting again Levi's habit of asking questions that assumed facts—I was impressed that he could so quickly intuit the truth. "But is there no alternative? Brewster says the medication makes him feel . . . strange."

"Tardive dyskinesia," Levi said, nodding his head. "Those uncontrollable movements you see, like jerking his arms for no reason, or when he rolls his tongue outside his mouth—it's a known side effect of *any* medication that controls . . . or even eliminates . . . the voices. Brewster's schizophrenia is what we call 'Undifferentiated.' He's not paranoid, he's not disorganized, and he's never had a catatonic episode. So Brewster has a real shot at functioning in the community. But he's got to achieve *and* maintain a consistent blood-level of his medications before he can participate in our skill-building program."

"What skills are taught?" I asked, genuinely curious.

"That depends on where we start. For some, it could be as basic as personal hygiene. Brewster actually has a relatively high GAF—" Seeing my obvious confusion, he explained: "Global Assessment of Functioning. The higher the better. Brewster could *already* handle a wide variety of clerical jobs, for example."

Sensing that Brewster did not resent being spoken of in this manner—indeed, he seemed to regard the information I was being given as praise—I asked, "Who would hire—?"

"That's another skill we teach," Levi said. "Job-finding. Handling the interview. How you *keep* a job. We do the same thing with housing, transportation . . . anything that gives the client a realistic shot at self-maintenance. Truth is, Brewster could have been on his own a long time ago, if he put some effort into it."

I looked at Brewster.

"I don't want a job," the young man finally admitted, blushing furiously. "I just want to work on my library."

"But you have to come here to get your check," Levi said. His voice was neutral, not accusatory. "So you show up and go through the motions."

"I come to every—"

"Yeah. You never miss a session," Levi said, his voice hardening slightly. "But you never *participate* in them, either."

"If it wasn't for my sister's husband—"

"You'd move in with her," Levi finished. "But what

would that change? You still wouldn't be taking care of yourself, Brewster; you'd just be changing caretakers."

"The meds make me all . . . fuzzy. I can't think straight. How could I ever hold a job?" Brewster said.

"I'm not saying it'd be easy," Levi told him. "I *never* said that, did I?"

"No . . ." Brewster replied, his attempt to divert the conversation away from his own lack of interest in what Levi had called self-maintenance having failed.

I waited a few moments, then I spoke into the silence: "Can you . . . can you tell me why Brewster might, most sincerely, believe he does not need this medication?"

"When a schizophrenic goes off medication, there's a honeymoon period," Levi told me. "His mood elevates, the kinetic tics occur less frequently, or even stop altogether. Off the meds, he gets all manic. Expansive, grandiose, absolutely convinced he's in total control of himself. Then comes the . . . episode."

"Always?"

"Always. No different than taking a diabetic off insulin and putting him on a diet of hot-fudge sundaes. We try to build in every option possible, and we're always adding new ones. But the medication, that one's nonnegotiable."

"You will reject Brewster if he does not—?"

"It's not personal," Levi cut me short. "Everybody here likes Brewster, and he knows it. But he *also* knows that ACT is all about helping folks change their lives, and, for some of our people, they can't even get *started* unless they commit to taking their medication. This isn't a Welfare office. Brewster's got himself a nice, certified diagnosis. He knows he can stop taking his meds and he'll still keep right on getting his Disability check. But he won't be picking it up here."

I shifted my posture so that I could triangulate Levi and Brewster, although I addressed my words only to Levi. "So Brewster has *chosen* to be in a program where more is required of him than he is willing to give?"

"Yeah," Levi said, leaning on his forearms. "I wonder about that myself."

"I like talking to Levi," Brewster said.

It was as if theater curtains were lifted, and the play was the revelation of a secret. I then understood the true reason why Brewster had asked me to accompany him that day. Despite his claims, some part of him *did* want to self-maintain. He attended the various programs at this place not because that was the only way to get his government stipend, but because it was his only channel to Levi.

"You are a young man to have acquired so much wisdom," I said to the therapist.

"I'm a good listener," he said, flashing a quick, thin smile.

"Ranger doesn't have to . . ." Brewster muttered sullenly.

Before I could act to protect Ranger's privacy, Levi had already stepped on Brewster's childish sulkiness: "The ACT Team works with the most high-need cases, but that's the *only* thing our clients have in common. You want to be treated as an individual, right, Brewster?"

"Sure. I mean—"

"I don't want to hear anything like that again, okay?"

"Levi," Brewster pleaded, "I didn't mean to—"

"Sure," Levi said. "Just let it go. Any decisions you make, you make them about *you,* okay?"

"Okay."

"Your expectations, they, too, vary with the individual?" I asked, sensing Brewster's anxiety at having trespassed across a known barrier.

"Right," Levi answered, his voice back to neutral, the very sound soothing to Brewster. "Let's say, hypothetically, there was a man with PTSD—Post-Traumatic Stress Disorder—as a result of a long period during which he was fighting for his own survival . . . like a soldier in combat. If his problem *was* due to military service, he'd be entitled to treatment at the VA. But we see a lot of guys who blame the government for whatever's going on in their heads. They end up here, because you couldn't ask for a less military outfit than this one."

How Levi assumed I knew Ranger, I did not know. But it was clear he was offering me the "hypothetical" information for a purpose. I immediately seized the opportunity to test the limits of my access.

"And if a person had, say, an addiction to gambling?"

"If that was his *real* problem, we'd probably never see him," Levi said. "Depending on his resources, he could get anything from celebrity spa 'rehab' to a bed in a detox facility, only it wouldn't be dope they were trying to get out of his system. Most of them end up in one of the self-help programs. Like AA."

"That contract you had me sign . . . ?"

"Yeah?"

"Could not Brewster sign one as well?"

"I'm not a lawyer," Levi said.

"Ah. Forgive my poor English," I said. "What I meant

was, you said each individual has a different level of . . . functioning, is it?"

"Uh-huh."

"And Brewster's is quite high?"

"It is."

"So I am not asking you a question about whether he could sign a contract to buy a house. My question is: Could Brewster sign the contract every man signs when he gives his word? Is he . . . functioning enough to do that?"

Levi gave me a hard, searching look. Then he said, "I wasn't lying when I told you I was a good listener."

I bowed.

He quickly turned to Brewster. "How many days, Brewster? No games. How many?"

"Five," the young man repeated, without hesitation.

"Counting today's?"

"Yes. But, Levi—"

"Which means we can cut that down to four. Understand? You come *here* to get your meds from now on, Brewster. Every day. We'll trust you over the weekends, give you three days' worth on Fridays. Same day you let us draw some blood."

"That's not—"

"Yeah, it's fair," Levi said. I could now detect a vein of well-controlled anger in his voice. "This is a place where we help people help themselves, Brewster. We're a therapeutic team, not a fucking pharmacy, got it?"

"I never said—"

"Your behavior said it for you. So that's the deal. You give us one solid month without missing a day, we go back to giving you a week's supply at a time. You come to the programs and you do more than just sit there, understand? *That's* our contract. You want to be a man, stand up and we'll shake on it. You don't, there's plenty of other places where you can go and pick up your check."

None of us moved for a long minute. Then Brewster stood up. He stuck out his hand. "I promise, Levi," he said.

"Good enough for me," Levi told him. He hit a button on his desk. "How can I—?" came through the telephone speaker.

"Pull one day's med package for Brewster," Levi said. "He'll be in once a day from now on, until I tell you different."

"Dr. Pkhafatsh's orders—"

"He doesn't work here, okay? He's just a rubber stamp," Levi interrupted. "If he's got a problem, he knows where to find me."

Levi pushed a button, and the speaker went silent.

I got to my feet, faced the therapist—I now knew the true meaning of the word—bowed, and said, "Would a true friend of Brewster's allow him to sell his medication?"

"Never," Levi said, holding my eyes with his own.

"So it shall be," I said, signing my own contract.

I followed Brewster to a window where he picked up a packet. After a moment's hesitation, he took a proffered plastic cup of water, and swallowed the pills he had poured into his hand.

We left the building together.

89

"You can't rush these things." Lamont spoke out of the side of his mouth as he continued to scan the street from a "fishing spot" we had claimed earlier that day.

Darkness had fallen. Thus, we had fewer competitors. And considerably less fish. But our presence would not be seen as remarkable; this city's streets are so thoroughly covered with those seeking money from strangers that only their absence would attract attention.

Although they all seek alms, few would regard themselves as beggars. Some stalk the subway cars, virtually *demanding* money as they loom over seated citizens. Some prefer the street, putting on "performances," such as singing or dancing or playing an instrument, an open receptacle nearby for passersby to reward their efforts. Some spend all day in front of hand-lettered signs that explain their plight. "Disabled Vet" was highly favored until recently, but has now largely been replaced by references to lost employment. Some stagger about, holding an empty cup, mumbling incoherently, glassy-eyed and drooling. Some reek of cheap wine. Some wander aimlessly, others have rigidly established routes. Occasionally, there are even physical battles over a particularly desirable location.

According to Michael, the city's homeless shelters are so overcrowded that people are often turned away. Lamont told me that today's shelters were just like the "dorms" he had been sentenced to as a youth. His description of those dorms was horrifying, but Lamont said they were considered a rite of passage for those who sought high status among youth gangs.

Silence fell between us, as it does when Lamont and I both need to search ourselves.

I thought of adaptation. Here, winter kills by its very presence. Some who cannot find shelter fall asleep and do not awaken. Were it not for our dugouts, desperate measures would have been required years ago.

"Watch that one," Lamont suddenly intruded, his chin tilted toward a dark-haired young woman in a shimmering red skirt that barely concealed her sex, and a matching band of the same material in lieu of a blouse. She was expertly navigating on extraordinarily high heels, weaving between the cars driving closest to the curb. The ones driving very slowly.

Perhaps ten minutes later, one of those cars came to a stop. The young woman walked over to it as its window slid down. She put her head and upper body inside the car, creating an exaggerated display of her buttocks. A moment later, she withdrew, and the car pulled off.

"Too rich for the boy's blood," Lamont said.

Before I could ask him to explain, another car had stopped. The young woman repeated the same gestures. But, this time, a bargain must have been struck, because she walked around to the far side of the car and climbed in.

"They're going to the Cheshire," Lamont said. "That's a trick hotel. Rooms by the hour. Girl like that, she won't be doing you in the front seat. You want that kind of action, you go over to the West Side. Cheaper meal, smaller menu."

I said nothing, watching similar choreography repeated by other young women.

"This is one of the best strolls in the city," Lamont told me. "At least, it is today. They move 'em around."

The young woman in the red outfit returned in less than an hour. She held a brief conversation with a blond woman, each of them smoking a cigarette. The blonde took a small cell phone from her purse and opened it, apparently answering a call. I could not hear whatever she said, but she seemed to be remonstrating with whoever the caller was.

Both women returned to their work. The girl in the red outfit was more consistent, but all succeeded in attracting customers.

It was getting quite late when a black sedan with lavish gold trim and oversized wheels of the same color pulled to the curb. It gleamed as if polished with oil.

Both girls scurried over to the car. They seemed to be competing for the attention of the driver, but the exchange was short, and the black sedan pulled away without either one inside.

"His game is weak," Lamont said. "That's old-style, checking your traps like that. A player who's got his game down, he don't need to be checking; he knows his ho's gonna bring him *his* money."

"So he is not the one we want?"

"He's *just* what we want, bro. Lightweight like him, he's gotta carry his flash with him. We're not gonna find some major-leaguer out here. A pimp on that level, his ass is parked in some club right this minute, snorting lines off a platinum spoon one of his women bought for him. What *we* want is a man who *wants* all that, but he's still dialing long-distance. Maybe he's too young, maybe he's new to the game—I don't know. But you saw his play, right? See how easy he'd be?"

"No."

"No?" Lamont said, apparently surprised at my response.

"He stopped only to converse with those women. Not only did they expect him, they might attempt to interfere with any attempt to rob him."

"That's what we need Michael's five C's for," Lamont said, his teeth showing in a lupine grin.

90

Over the next several days, our band developed separate schedules. Although Lamont, Target, and I rose with the others, we would only go far enough to find a place to continue sleeping until afternoon. This is more difficult than it might first appear, but it is really no great achievement when the weather is warm, especially to those who have been forced to learn this city as our kind have.

This new schedule was necessary because our surveillance required that we be awake and alert until approximately four in the morning. Each time we departed, I would note that, as if in obedience to some unspoken law, the streets themselves had taken the coming of dawn as a command to change ownership.

The deeper the darkness, the more the streets had belonged to the predators. Despite the artificiality of human predation, an organic food chain always imposed itself.

When I told Lamont what I had discovered, he simply shrugged. Seeing that I would not accept one of his "that's just the way it is" explanations, he pointed out that the prostitutes we watched would prey upon a customer only opportunistically. "A good whore'll work some plastic out of the trick's pocket the second he uses the bathroom. Swipe it in two seconds. He won't catch wise until he sees some big-ass charges on his bill. Not *too* big, though—that'd force his hand, blow the deal."

"Deal? Would such a . . . customer not be a victim?"

"It don't work like that, Ho. He's giving up something, but he's getting something, too. He doesn't make a squawk about the money, and his wife never learns where he was the night the charges got rung up. A whore who doesn't get too greedy's got nothing to worry about."

Yet, despite Lamont's explanation, I could not regard the women as the skillful exploiters he depicted. It did not require in-depth knowledge of being a "sex worker"—Luzanne had always referred to herself as such—to realize that each woman was taking unimaginable risks each time she entered a stranger's car. When I asked how the male's risk of losing money could ever be balanced against the female's risk of losing her life, Lamont had no more to contribute than: "That's the game, Ho. Always has been; always will be."

Perhaps the natural balance lies unseen. The men who profit by the dangerous labor of such women could themselves be prey, I thought, as the screen of my mind displayed the murky image of a white car rolling to a stop next to our dugouts.

As dawn broke, the morning light would herald the influx of the new owners of the streets. Among those, dress and mannerisms clearly delineated status—some were the masters of huge buildings, others cleaned those buildings. Often, they would pass one another, moving in opposite directions, one having finished his labors, the other about to begin.

While I continued to focus on the two women, calculating distances and angles, I noticed that Lamont's attention was constantly shifting to our left, to the end of the block. It was that corner around which the pimp's distinctive car would come each night.

"No way he's gonna cruise Lex in that ride, Ho," Lamont said. "He cribs uptown, I'm thinking. So he jumps on the FDR, and comes across at the exit, see?"

I did not.

"Never mind, bro. Look, hold the fort, okay? I gotta go scout Triple-A for prospects."

With that, Lamont stood up and shuffled his way down the street. No actor could have portrayed a shambling drunk more convincingly.

91

Three more nights passed before Lamont said, "Time to buy our supplies. I figure two and a quarter should do it." He rose to his feet and walked toward the corner. This time, his gait was steady and purposeful—a man on his way to work.

When he returned, he said, "This is our last night here, Ho. We can go home now. Tomorrow, we set up in a new spot."

We arrived at the dugout much earlier than we had for several days. Only Brewster was there.

"You guys still scoping out the job?" he asked, his voice once more a reflection of the heroes of his treasured books.

"Nope," Lamont said, confidently. "We're ready to go."

"You need another gun?"

"We're okay, bro."

Brewster smiled. It was a relaxed, genuine smile. He seemed at peace with his parallel world. It was only then that I understood "another gun" to mean "a helping hand." And that Lamont's respectful refusal was taken not as an insult, but as vindication.

Brewster had been keeping his contract.

"My sister says I can come back first thing this morning," he told us. "Gonna take a while, she's way the hell out in Queens. So I better get in the wind."

"That is a good plan," I said.

92

Knowing Michael and Ranger could return at any time, I turned to Lamont. "And what is *our* plan?"

"Where we've been setting up shop the last few nights, you know what's just around the corner from there, Ho?"

"More prostitutes?"

Lamont lit a cigarette, studying my face as he did so. My friend guarded his power of irony zealously; he would not appreciate seeing it displayed by others. His slight nod communicated his belief in the innocence of my question.

"Sure," he said. "What else? But Lex is off-limits to those girls—that'd be working without a net."

"You mean, those women, they have no pimps?"

"They *all* have pimps," Lamont said. "I don't care if

they're blowing guys in an alley for a buck, if they're on the game street-level, they got some kinda pimp. But, like I told you before, there's pimps and there's pimps. Our guy, he's up there, but not top-shelf, okay?"

I nodded. When I taught, I had always emphasized that there was only one true universal measurement—combat. High proficiency in one style would only apply *to* that style. This is why sporting contests have highly specific rules—a Shodokan tournament would not permit Muay Thai knee strikes; a boxer may not kick his opponent. My students were told never to accept a challenge, because a duel is no different from a tournament. My system was designed for the reality of life. And life has no rules.

Ah, yes . . . *my* system.

I told Chica she was ready. That indictment never left my thoughts. It stabbed at my arrogance, always drawing blood.

"What I've been checking out is this one girl working around that corner. Lot of miles on her, maybe, but she still got plenty of bounce to the ounce," Lamont continued. "But not enough to get her a stall in a top player's stable."

"Would not her experience—?"

"*Nailed* it, bro. That's what she *should* be doing, schooling the fresh turn-outs. But those sorry-ass pimps they got out there now, all they think about is, how much cash am I gonna get *tonight*? The way I read her, this girl, she got too much pride to be last in line.

"But that's not how I came on to her. First, I had to give her the quarter for five minutes of her time. She was a little spooked—and not the way you think," he said, grinning. "But I told her we could talk right there—she never had to step down no alley or nothing—so she listened."

Still, I waited.

"This tells the story," Lamont said, as he held up two halves of a hundred-dollar bill.

"Where is the other bill?" I asked.

"This is *both,* Ho. Right here. And Mercy—that's our blonde—she's got both, too. I showed her the pair of C-notes, told her what she'd have to do to earn them.

"Being a natural-born whore, she wanted the money up front. But I was hustling before she was born, and I know how to deal with that.

"So now we're each holding half. No good to her; no good to me. The deal is, she gets the other half soon as she opens the window for us to slip in."

"Now I am lost," I acknowledged.

"A pimp only stays in business if he can keep pulling new girls," Lamont told me. "Some do turn-outs—sweet-talk a country girl into just turning a couple of little tricks until she gets herself together. You got some broads been out here for years, still telling themselves their man is putting all the money away so they can open a business or whatever. 'Just till we get on our feet, baby.' Only they never get off their backs.

"Then you got your gorillas. Snatch some runaway kid, torture her until she goes along. Those ain't pimps, no matter what they call themselves.

"There's other ways—ship the girls in from China or Mexico or wherever, keep them locked up until they get used up. Or scumbags who rent out their own kids. But you won't see those girls on the street—the people who own them, they can't take the chance."

Lamont lit another cigarette, studying the glowing tip as if it held secrets.

"Just think of sharks, okay? You know their deal—keep swimming or die. For a pimp, it's either keep getting new stuff or you're out of the game.

"Lots of ways to do that, like I said. But the *prize* would be a girl who's already in The Life. You don't have to school her; she knows what to do and how to do it. The best ones, they're like stars. And stars got egos, and they'll always listen to a sales pitch. So a good pimp, he's always out there, trolling for a new catch."

"Would not the pimp who originally—?"

"No, bro. You know what a girl in The Life calls it, when she gets with a pimp? She says, 'I *chose* him.' It's that feeling that keeps them working. A top player *expects* girls to come and go. Chase after a girl who walks away, you lose a lot of face behind that kind of punk move. A real player holds a woman with his mind, not his hands.

"The guy we want, that's what he wants to be—a real player. Top-shelf. And now we got ourselves some bait."

"This woman . . . Mercy?"

"Oh yeah."

"She is going to convince this pimp—"

"Jesus!" Lamont said. "Whores don't be *convincing* pimps of nothing. She's gonna flag him down, just like he was a trick. But, see, he's gonna know what's happening—she's *asking* to be pulled, saying she wants to step up in class. No way our boy's not gonna call her over, get a closer look at the goods."

"And that is when—"

"*Exactly* when," Lamont said. "All Mercy's got to do is get his car to stop. When he opens his window to rap to her, that's *our* window opening, too. You take the pimp, I take the wheel, and we just drive down to the river. While he's still out, we grab his cash and fade. What's he gonna do when he comes around, call the cops?"

"But he will know it was this woman—"

"You think he's ever gonna find *her* ass anywhere around here after that? That's why she's so perfect, Ho. We've been talking, her and me. She's been around long enough. Ain't nothing stupid about that woman. She's gonna flip the script. Find some little town where the wannabes are young boys, just starting out. A woman like her, she'd be gold to a man like that. I figure she's on the Greyhound before we even get back to our place."

"Place! Case! Trace! Face!" Target chanted.

"He cannot hunt us," I assured Target. "Lamont will be just another homeless drunk in his eyes. And he will never see me at all."

"Rehearsal time," Lamont announced, and began drawing lines in the dirt with a sharp-edged stick.

93

"Don't you need some . . . stuff?" Lamont asked me.

"For what purpose?"

"Hell, bro, I don't know. I thought you guys had all kinds of special gear."

"Lamont," I said, using his name to indicate I was growing weary of his circumlocutions, "we do not have much time before Ranger and Michael return. . . ."

"Ninja gear, Ho. You know, like one of those black bodysuits and hoods and all."

"How many times have I—?"

"Right. You ain't no ninja. I got it, okay? I just thought . . ."

"That I have been lying?" I asked, heartsick that my friend would think such of me.

"You? Come on, Ho. I just thought you were being . . . humble. You know, like you're always saying."

"Thank you," I said, with sincerity. "Perhaps I have preached humility to the point where it has become a form of posturing."

"Fuck me! I can't do this. Look, Ho, I just want to know. Whatever it is, I'm down with it. Down with *you.* But you're always doing stuff it don't look like you *can* do, you see what I mean? Look, I know this ain't the goddamned movies, all right? I was just trying to help, man."

"Ho! Know! Ho! Know!" Target erupted, not only introducing a new pattern to his outbursts, but speaking softly, too.

I centered myself, realizing that our plan would put something far more precious than money at stake.

To gain trust, one must give trust.

"A true ninja would be as a true samurai, Lamont. As you said, life is not a movie. Both ninja and samurai have this in common: they serve a master. Their sword is for hire. They train until a level of skill is reached, then they seek employment with the family of their fathers. In Japan, the concept of loyalty is always the same: the servant, by whatever name, is loyal to the master. In ancient times, if the master were to die, it was expected that his servants respond in order of rank. A maid would seek other employment. A samurai would commit seppuku . . . ritual suicide."

"Damn."

"But a highly skilled assassin is also highly employable. Instead of choosing seppuku, many became ronin . . . unattached to any master. Some might search for another to serve. But others would serve only themselves.

"If you see a parallel between this and organized criminal enterprises all around the world, you would be correct. In Japan, however, the concept extended to every level of society. A 'salaryman' would be called such because he would be expected to start with a company as a young man, and never leave. His life is secure. However, were he to be caught even *inquiring* about working for another company, he would be disgraced. Shunned. As the Indians have their 'untouchables,' so the Japanese would regard a salaryman who had strayed."

"So, if some big company went bankrupt, what were these guys supposed to do, jump off a bridge?"

"Many did," I told him. "There will always be those who place security above freedom. When that security—their master, and all he represents—is gone, they commit the final act of what they believe to be loyalty. It would not matter whether their master was a shogun or a business executive.

"But those times have passed. The pendulum has swung

in the opposite direction. The one-way loyalty of the past has been replaced by the one-way loyalty of today."

"Me first," Lamont said.

"Yes."

"That's why you're always saying we need each other, right?"

"Yes."

"So it doesn't matter, labels," Lamont said, dragging deeply on his cigarette. "Once, I was a poet—"

He raised his hand to prevent me from interrupting as I was about to, then continued. "What I mean is, when people *called* me a poet, I called myself a poet. When they stopped, I stopped. But, like you told me a long time ago, I'm what I always was."

"A man may possess the tools to build a house, yet allow them to rust on the ground he sleeps on."

"You are what you do," Lamont said, almost reverently.

"Hai!"

"I *was* a lot of things. Now I'm not any of them. But I can still use what I learned from *being* those things, like how I'm setting up this job. Hell, like *I* was saying about Mercy. That's what you're saying, right, Ho?"

"No."

"No!? Then what the—?"

"Possessions take their value from how we value *them*. Brewster's library may have some commercial value, but he would not sell it for any sum of money. Ranger treasures the compass you obtained for him far beyond its cash value. And you ask me to use my skills, Lamont. Not to gain something for myself, but to protect one of our own."

"You wouldn't do it for yourself anyway, Ho."

"I would not," I agreed, thinking of what Levi had taught me. "I will return to . . . a place in my past, so that our . . . our family can continue. I do not consider this a sacrifice; it is my duty. What, then, is yours?"

"Mine? This whole thing is mine, Ho. I'm going back, too."

"You are not," I told him. "There is but one way for you to go back, yet you refuse to walk that path."

"What do you want me to do, brother? Start writing again?" he said, as if describing an impossibility.

"Where else *are* you, Lamont? Where is your true self?"

"I gave up—"

"As a youth, you engaged in battle many times. Did you ever consider surrendering to the enemy?"

"Man . . ."

"Your true self was a warlord then. Later, your true self became a poet. What else is abandoning your true self *but* surrendering?"

I reached inside my coat. My fingers found what I had carried with me for many years. My precious notebook, survivor of flames. I handed it to my friend.

Lamont opened the notebook. On its first page was my haiku.

I gently took the book from his hands, tore out that first page, and handed the newly virginal book back to its rightful owner.

94

“What did they wear those suits for, anyway?” Lamont asked me the next evening.

I could tell he was talking to calm himself. Lamont had abstained from liquor for many days. His initial tremors had passed, but so had his usual calm, ironic demeanor. None of us had commented on this.

“Who?”

“Ninjas, man. I mean, they *did* have those costumes and all, for real, right?”

“Camouflage is a weapon. If one *becomes* the darkness . . .”

“And *I’m* the one who’s always saying they never see us.” Lamont reached into his inside pocket and withdrew the leather notebook. Without taking his eyes off the street, he quickly scribbled some words with a soft-pointed pen. I could see tiny blue sparks as his hand crackled with the power of what it was recording.

95

Two nights later, we were in position. Lamont saw the black sedan before I did. “Game time,” he said, an unmistakable lilt of happiness in his whispered voice.

“Go back,” I said to Target. He opened his mouth to clang. I held my finger to my lips. “Now!” I said.

Still Target would not move. “We will come back to our home,” I promised. “Very soon. You must wait for us.”

The woman Lamont called Mercy stepped out of the shadows. She strode purposefully to the curb, switching her hips as if testing her balance. She made some fluttering gesture with her left hand.

The black sedan slowly glided to a stop.

The passenger-side window slid down.

Mercy walked toward the sedan, presenting herself as an expensive piece of jewelry to a valued customer.

As she bent forward, Lamont stumbled into her, doing his Bowery-bum act. He bumped Mercy aside, saying, "Help a brother out, player." I reached through the opened window on the driver's side and stabbed a nerve block into the pimp's exposed neck with two fingers as I rolled my thumb to the junction point on his spine.

I climbed inside and pushed the unconscious pimp up against the passenger door, my eyes on the street. I caught a brief glimpse of Mercy as she scurried back into the darkness.

Lamont slipped behind the wheel, as relaxed as if the car was his own. As we pulled away, the passenger-side window closed silently. The glass was deeply tinted.

96

We reached the underpass without incident, in even less time than Lamont had promised.

"Got to shake it now, bro."

"The police—?"

"Down here? Nah. But this ride, it's a body lying out on the desert. Take a little time for the vultures to make sure it's safe to make their move, but they're gonna be circling pretty soon. Come on."

As Lamont went through the pimp's clothing, I opened the glove compartment. It was empty except for a cell phone, some papers, and a small pearl-handled pistol.

"Pimp piece," Lamont said, looking up from his work. "Probably a punk-ass twenty-five. But it could be worth something. Snatch it, Ho. But don't *touch* that cell—it could be on some cop's track list."

Lamont removed a good deal of jewelry, including a very large wristwatch and several chains, before he extracted a thick roll of bills, wrapped in an elastic band.

"Meet you back at the spot," he said, my cue to exit the car. We had previously agreed to return separately, by different routes. Although it was highly unlikely our crime would have been reported by a bystander, should this have occurred, the police would be looking for a two-person team. I had asked if we were not also putting Mercy in danger, but Lamont only laughed. "Only trace they gonna find of *that* blonde is a wig in an alley."

97

When I returned to the dugout, Lamont was already there. Sitting with his back to a wooden beam, Target very close to him.

Michael and Ranger were also there, but they were quite obviously giving Lamont a wide berth.

I approached. Lamont would not look up. I sat across from him. I regret that, for a moment, I thought he had celebrated our success by getting drunk. But when he met my eyes, I saw only pain.

"I thought I still knew the game, Ho. I thought I was still with it."

"What is wrong, Lamont?"

"Me, that's what's wrong," he said, in a voice too full of sorrow for mere sobs to express.

"But we were—"

"Oh, we pulled it off, all right," he said, bitterly. "Only what I thought was a player on his way up was nothing but an all-front, two-bit simp."

"Why would that—?"

For answer, Lamont tossed the roll of bills he had taken from the pimp's unconscious body into my lap.

"That's a Kansas City bankroll you're holding, Ho. Go on, pull the cover off."

I removed the elastic band. The first three bills were hundreds; the remainder were all fives and singles.

"You see this?" Lamont said, holding up the gold chains. "Probably ten-K . . . or even plate. That car . . . it's probably a fucking rental the punk slapped some rims on. That little pistol you got? *That* was probably our biggest fucking score."

"All of this . . . ?"

"*With* the cash, maybe five yards, total," Lamont said, his voice threatening to break. "I thought we'd clear a few thou, easy."

"You can never be sure—" Michael started to say, until a look from Lamont froze his words. Whether Michael was attempting to comfort Lamont or philosophize about gambling did not matter—either would have been a dangerous error.

"I'm old, Ho," Lamont said.

"Old! Cold! Bold! Told!"

"Target speaks the truth," I said, without inflection. "Your knowledge and skills have not deserted you, my brother. The world around you has changed—you are what you always have been."

"Yeah? Back in the day—"

"Which day, Lamont? The day when you were a gang leader? Or the day you discovered you were a poet?"

"You wrote a fucking *book,* man!" Ranger said.

I nodded in Ranger's direction, grateful for his support. "How many could say such?" I asked Lamont. "But that, too, is meaningless . . . compared with the book you have yet to write."

"You're old enough to be my fucking grandfather, Ho. But you can still—"

"I can still do what is in me, Lamont."

Lamont buried his face in his hands. Target moved close to him. So close their shoulders were touching.

98

I was awake before sunrise to find Lamont sitting next to me.

"Give me the piece, Ho."

"The pistol?"

"Yeah."

"It is gone," I told him, deliberately looking out over the water where Michael had seen the white woman in the white mink coat climb out of the white Rolls-Royce and throw what he believed was our "mortal lock" into the river.

"Are you nuts?" Lamont said, indignantly. "I already said we could get some money for it."

"You did not want it to sell."

Lamont went silent.

Target joined us.

"How did you know?" Lamont finally said.

"I learned from you," I told my brother. "You once explained that selling a firearm was insane, because it might have been used in crimes. If the purchaser were to be captured with it, fear of prosecution would immediately make him identify whoever he bought it from."

In fact, I had been present when Lamont *had* disdainfully rejected an offer to buy a pistol for the price of a bottle of liquor, saying, "Fucking thing's probably got half-a-dozen murders on it, fool!"

But Lamont had not wanted the pimp's gun to sell; he had wanted to redeem himself, ignoring all the reasons he had given Brewster for not attempting an armed robbery. *Better a warrior's death,* I felt his thoughts inside of me.

"Yeah," he said, slowly. "Yeah, I remember. Gotta start listening to my own rap, huh?"

"Others would listen as well," I said to my brother, reaching over to touch his heart, tapping the exact spot where he now kept his leather notebook.

99

Although I had not precisely spoken an untruth, I had deliberately allowed Lamont to believe that I had removed the pistol from his pocket as he slept and thrown it into the river. Had I told Lamont that I had no idea what could have happened to the pistol, the balance of our band would have been disrupted—perhaps permanently—by any search for it.

100

Later that same morning, I went to see Levi. Lamont came with me without stating his reasons; Target came because he had grown accustomed to being with Lamont and myself over the course of the past weeks.

The receptionist was guardedly polite.

I asked if I might be allowed to speak with Levi.

To the receptionist's series of questions, I responded: "This concerns one of his . . ." I hesitated, not knowing how those such as Brewster were referred to. Quickly, I decided, and finished with ". . . cases."

"You're not from another agency," the receptionist stated, not impolitely, but in a tone that clearly communicated that I would not be permitted access.

"Kid's on the verge," Lamont interjected. "Figured his worker would want to know, but if you all don't—"

"Would you please sit over there and wait?" the receptionist said. "I'll get someone to help you."

We were barely seated when the woman who had been introduced to me as Glo entered the room, looked around briefly, then walked directly over to me.

"Who?" is all she said.

"We are here about Brewster," I told her. "I have met with Levi before."

"Is that right?" she asked, just as the large black man came up behind her.

"Came in with him a while back," the black man said. "Your name, it's Ho, am I saying it right?"

"Yes." I bowed. "And yours is Earl, I believe."

A wide smile split his face. "Come on," he said.

Lamont and Target rose as one. Earl turned to face them.

"Anything I can do for you guys?"

"They are with me," I explained.

"Pretty small offices back there," he said.

"We don't take up much room," Lamont snapped back, deliberately staring at Earl's massive frame. "And we're not going to set off any metal detectors."

They exchanged looks. Then Earl extended his hand, palm-up. Lamont slapped it. Earl turned and gestured for us to follow.

This time, he brought us into a much larger room, mostly filled by a large table and a number of mismatched chairs. Following his gesture, we all seated ourselves—including the woman.

As Earl left the room, the woman said, "I'm Gloria."

I rose, bowed, said, "I remember. We have met before. I am Ho. This is Lamont. And this is our friend Target."

"And you're here about Brewster?"

"Yes," I said. "I apologize if I am not addressing you correctly; I do not know your title."

"We don't do titles here, Mr. Ho."

"Then may I be 'Ho'?"

"Sure," she said, smiling slightly. Her eyes were neither

wary nor friendly—not communicators, but measuring instruments.

Levi and Earl came in together.

I again introduced each of us. Levi sat directly across from us, while Earl took the chair to our right, and Gloria remained on our left, closest to the door.

"Brewster has kept to his contract?" I began.

"You could set your clock by him," Earl affirmed.

Gloria nodded in agreement.

"That what you wanted?" Levi asked me.

"No," I said, carefully. "It was but a . . . prerequisite to my request. If Brewster had not been faithful to his contract, I would have no right to make that request."

"Break that down," Earl said.

"Ho backed the man's play," Lamont answered. "Brewster don't keep his word, it's like Ho didn't keep his. You can't trust a man's word, how you gonna deal with him?"

"Sometimes—" Gloria started to say.

"Begging your pardon, ma'am," Lamont interrupted, "but we ain't no . . . patients, or clients, or whatever. Ho may be older than sin, but he's sharp as a razor," he said, glancing at Earl. "Me, I'm a hardcore alkie, but I ain't no wet-brain. We're here about Brewster. If you can't trust us, ain't no point in us talking."

"What's up with Brewster?" Levi asked. "You implied that he might be . . ."

"I apologize for the ruse," I said. "Brewster is perhaps not suicidal. But he *is* facing a crisis. If it is not resolved, his ability to . . . deal with that would be very doubtful."

"He'd stop taking his meds?" Levi asked.

"No," I answered. "With all respect, if this crisis is not resolved, I believe the medication would lose its power to stop *him.*"

101

My explanation was lengthy and detailed, interrupted only when I said, "Brewster may live in a . . . parallel world. But that world has its own code. Brewster would not tell a lie."

"Lie! Cry! Die! Try!" Target clanged.

I could actually see a lightning burst of communication flickering between Gloria, Levi, and Earl. Their faces showed no reaction to Target's outburst, so I finished my account.

"This would have to be a staff call," Levi said, when I had concluded. "We're a team."

"I thought you were Brewster's . . . therapist," I said, deliberately not mentioning how Earl had referred to him as "boss" when I had visited before.

"I am," Levi replied. "But you're asking the whole team to take a risk, not just me."

"ACT?"

"That's right. And there's a lot of us. We all do different jobs, but we all do the same job."

"I understand," I told him, thinking of how our own tribe functioned.

"We can always help a client relocate . . ." Earl mused out loud.

"Brewster's not a housing client," Gloria said. Her tone was not that of a corrector, more like a comrade pointing out an obstacle to a plan.

"That's paperwork," Levi told them both. Turning to me, he said, "You're asking for manpower to move the books, a van to move them, plus—"

"I apologize for any confusion my poor language skills may have caused," I told them. "Such tasks are our responsibility, and ours alone. What we ask is for your assistance in housing Brewster's library."

"What's the diff—?"

"We're not running a game," Lamont interrupted Earl. "Ho's telling it just like it is. Getting the books out, that's on us. But there's gotta be a place where the kid can come and visit his stuff. Otherwise . . ."

"What about down in the basement, next to the boiler?" Gloria said.

"He could only come when we're open," Earl quickly joined her, as if appealing to Levi. "And he's *supposed* to be in some of the programs anyway."

"Has he not?" I asked.

Both Earl and Gloria looked puzzled, but Levi understood at once. "He hasn't missed since he signed our contract."

I bowed.

"I wasn't raised to be wasting space," Earl said. "That basement's just sitting there. . . ."

Levi nodded.

"Brewster could bring a friend on occasion," I said, not making it a question. "I am certain he would feel much more confident if he did not have to come alone."

I knew, even as I spoke, that Brewster had been visiting Levi for years. I knew that this ACT building was one place where Brewster *did* feel confident—a word others would translate as "safe."

Target opened his mouth . . . then snapped it shut, as if fearing what would emerge.

"Come back tomorrow," Levi told us.

102

"I need some clothes," Michael said that evening.

"It will not be cold for many—"

"Not for that," Michael cut short my speech, as if he knew I was concerned about a loss of focus with such a complex task facing us all.

"A fish in the water; a leaf on a tree," Ranger said. "Who should know that better than you, Ho?"

My mind struggled with what seemed to be Ranger interpreting Michael's bizarre request by quoting some principle of guerrilla warfare. If Ranger had retreated to the world where his insanity had been born, Michael would be the last person he would view as a comrade.

I sought calm within myself. Brewster and Target were inert objects. Lamont's eyes were silent—he was smoking as methodically as a carpenter driving a nail.

All that came to me was the phrase I had taught myself when I first began my new path: "Please forgive my ignorance. I do not understand."

"Michael's on recon," Ranger said. "He's got to blend, see?"

"Camouflage of some kind?"

"Bingo! He talks the lingo *perfect,*" Ranger said, as if

Michael had mastered a foreign language so completely that he could converse idiomatically. "He already looks like them, too."

"The white Rolls," Michael said. "There just *can't* be that many of them, right? Like we first . . ."

I nodded, more to keep Michael talking than because I was able to follow what he and Ranger seemed to assume I already understood.

"Okay," Michael said, in a brisk, self-assured tone. "Now stay with me, Ho. Times are tough. That's hard for us to see, from where we are. But the economy is tanking. Giant corporations going belly-up, all the loans are getting called in, and people can't pay up. Foreclosures everywhere you look. That's where that whole 'trickle-down' crap turns around and bites you in the ass. When we're in a boom, everybody's got money. Or *thinks* they do, anyway. But when we're going the other way, that trickles down, too. *Way* down."

"How does this—?"

"I keep in touch," Michael said, glancing at Lamont, as if preparing to ward off an attack.

Seeing no reaction, Michael continued, "I don't mean I've still got friends in the business. I burned through them. Everybody on this earth who ever liked me, or trusted me, or believed in me . . . gone."

"Not here," I said.

"You think I don't know that?" Michael said. "You think I don't know what this"—he spread his hands wide, as if to include us all—"is worth? Yeah, well, I don't blame you, if that's what you think. But you'd be wrong, Ho."

I sat, a student awaiting his teacher's next words.

"You know when I stopped . . . what I was doing, Ho? You know when I actually stopped? It wasn't after my wife left me. It wasn't after my kids—yeah, I've got kids; two of them—it wasn't after my kids disappeared from my life. Not even after I lost my last job, tapped out my last friend, hocked everything I had. Not after I stole everything I could. Then I got my ribs kicked in for . . . it doesn't matter. You know what I'm saying. You know I've been . . . doing it anyway. A little bet here, a lottery ticket, even dice-on-a-blanket when I got a little ahead."

"The white Rolls—?"

"That was the same thing," Michael said. "It *looked* better. That 'sure thing' I've been chasing ever since I . . . started. But we all know what would happen if that played out. Money. Fucking money. Big deal.

"We could all use money, but it wouldn't change anything. You *had* money, didn't you, Ho? We'd still all be what we were. And you know what I'd do with my share."

"Start a new streak," Lamont said, very quietly.

"That's right," Michael agreed. "A new losing streak. It wasn't until we had to save Brewster's library that I started thinking. Really thinking. But my mind's all . . . twisted. Look what I did. You think I'm proud of asking Ranger to get me the money to play that horse?"

"Hey, we're buddies," Ranger said. "You'd do the same for me."

Michael's eyes filled with tears. "Buddies. That's right. And a man doesn't *use* his buddies. I learned that from you, Ho. I learned that. I apologized to Ranger," he said, looking over at his friend. "But even as the words came out of my mouth, I knew I was the same fucking miserable low-life lying fraud I always was."

"Nah, bro," Ranger said. "You stepped up when they called your number."

"Man's saying it true," Lamont added.

"You know what they're talking about, Ho? Sure you do. I told myself I was just trying to get us a stake, so we could carry out the mission. But, in my mind, I was going to—"

"All that matters is what you *did* do," I told him.

"And *that's* when I stopped," Michael said, putting his face in his hands.

None spoke as Michael sobbed. Ranger got up and stood behind him, one hand on each of Michael's shoulders.

Finally, Michael looked up. "I haven't even . . . I can't explain it. But ever since I turned over the money, I stopped being a degenerate gambler. It's not . . . in me anymore. I don't . . . see things the way I did."

"Your spirit was stronger than the invader."

"I didn't *have* a spirit," Michael said. "It doesn't matter what you call things. I could walk away now. I mean it. I could just walk away. I know how to play the game. Sign up for some program, stop being a fucking 'addict,' turn myself into a real success story. Maybe even . . . talk to my kids again, someday."

"It is for this that you need the clothing—?"

"Get with the program, Ho," Lamont admonished me. "Michael don't need some fine vines to walk away; he needs them so he can *stay*."

"So the white Rolls-Royce, it is . . . ?"

"It's still our ticket out of this mess," Michael said, very carefully, not a trace of the salesman in his speech. "There's money in that car. *Our* money. Enough money to . . . do things. Things like Brewster's library. And those things, they're something *I* can do."

103

I did not sleep that night. Relentlessly, I examined myself. Time spent is not distance covered. All these years in the world I had chosen, and how close had I come to true atonement? Arrogance no longer ruled my life . . . but it still lurked within my spirit. Not daring to face my sword, it reached out its tendrils very tentatively, always testing. Each time I recognized its emergence, I struck.

But if the task is to uproot, the finest sword is still inferior to the crudest hoe.

At that moment, I became a seer. I viewed the future as clearly as if I were watching through a window. Even as I did, I understood this gift was not mine to keep; it was a temporary loan from the gods.

I saw Michael, free of his demons. He would never find his magical automobile, his need for such a savior gone. I saw Lamont standing before a small audience, reading aloud. I saw Brewster guaranteed safe passage to the world that comforted him, guided there by those who cared for him. I saw Ranger connected to others, back in "The World." I realized that those who cared for him could not alter what had been implanted. Their goal was not to change Ranger, but to keep him safe . . . and others safe from him. They accepted this.

As should I.

Before my vision left me, I asked, "And what of Target?" No answer came. Target had appeared among us as if formed by the elements. What led him to us was never known—one day he was among us, as though he had always been there. Where would Target walk if he were forced to walk alone?

I am an old man. Someday, I must leave.

To leave Target behind would be an unforgivable act. And most especially so for a man whose quest was to make himself worthy of forgiveness for the sin of desertion.

104

In the morning, I gathered our band. Quickly, we moved away from the dugouts.

None questioned where we were going, but the air around us was heavily charged, as if just after a rainstorm.

We gathered near the Hudson River, in the same area we used for sharing meals during the day. Along the way, we had made brief stops for provisions at various places where we knew recently discarded food would be waiting. With the exception of Lamont's coffee, we paid for nothing.

"I have a plan," I told the others. "It is in two stages, one to follow the other. For this to work, we must operate in teams."

I had expected questions. Instead, I felt only their attentiveness. There was no time for selfish pondering as to the meaning of this, so I continued.

"I will attempt to make certain arrangements," I said. "Only if I succeed can we then begin the plan. For the first stage, the teams will be myself and Ranger, Brewster and Target, and Lamont and Michael."

Still no questions, but I could sense the impending balance disruption among those I addressed. A change was coming, and any such prospect always frightens those of our tribe.

"For the final stage, the teams will be two. Myself and Lamont will be one; Michael, Brewster, Target, and Ranger will be the other."

Silence was their response.

"Only if I am able to make the arrangements I hope for can we act," I repeated. "But we must be certain of the second stage now. May I explain?"

"Come on with it," Lamont said, sipping from his coffee.

105

"A solid chute's no good," Ranger said, a few moments later. "Brewster's the only one that can get up there, right?"

"Until there is more room, yes," I agreed. "But once a certain number of the books are offloaded . . ."

"Load! Code! Road! Load!" Target erupted.

"Yes," I said. "Brewster, once there is room, you could return and show Target how to enter your library. From there, he could assist you mightily."

"That'd be aces with me," Brewster said.

"That's why you can't go with a solid chute," Ranger said, his mind fully attuned to the task. "What we need is cargo netting. It's light enough for Brewster to carry—I'll show you how to back-wrap, bro—it won't make a sound when you drop it, and it won't catch no light, either."

"That is a far superior plan to what I had envisioned," I said. "My plan . . ." It was then I caught myself, and said, "I should say, of course, *our* plan—were it not for Target, we never would have realized it was a chute we needed to begin with—is vastly improved. Can we obtain . . . ?"

"Army surplus," Ranger interrupted. "I know a place. One-man show. All he watches out for is the expensive stuff. Michael can take the guy off to one side—I'll clue him what to say—and I'll have what we need in a minute."

"I can grab the man's eye, too," Lamont added. "Michael goes in, starts his rap. Then me, walking around, looking at stuff. Guess who's gonna be under the evil eye? You can ghost right in then, bro."

"Diversion. Roger that!" Ranger barked out.

"Brewster, what are your plans for this morning?"

"I was going to see Levi. But if—"

"No, that would be perfect," I said. "Target, will you accompany Brewster while I attempt to make the arrangements for the use of a van? If you were to be with me, it would make those I must bargain with unwilling to negotiate."

Target got up and then sat down next to Brewster. But something in his eyes as he regarded me caused me to amplify my last sentence. "It would not be *you* that would disturb these people, Target," I said. "They are very rigid individuals, and any alteration of protocol would be . . . unsettling to them. It is not who I bring, it is that I would not be coming alone that they would deem a breach of manners. The meeting must be only between two."

Nothing showed on Target's face. I had never before asked him to accompany only one of us, knowing he feared the number two, which I had deliberately just emphasized. His mouth twitched, but no sound emerged.

"Let us all go, then," I said. "We will meet behind Brewster's library just before darkness falls. Are we agreed?"

I waited patiently. Hearing no response, I stood up and finally began the walk I had once believed I had started the day I left my old life behind.

106

"Pull up to the gate," Levi told me. "Flash the lights on the van twice. Not high-low; on-off."

"My gratitude—"

"It's just a few hours more overtime that we can't bill for," Earl said, his voice conveying the message that such was not an infrequent occurrence for the ACT Team.

"Is he going to be all worked up?" Gloria asked me.

"I would think the opposite," I told her. "Brewster will be—"

"Not Brewster," she said. "Ranger."

"The mission will be over."

"Yours, maybe," she said. "It doesn't matter—I take him as he comes, and he never makes appointments, anyway."

107

I showed the restaurant owner the message I had carefully drawn on the stiff piece of white cardboard he had provided.

"This is a most serious statement."

"Hai."

"It cannot be placed on the window glass. That would make it apparent that—"

"This sign states a personal grievance only," I said.

He sat in silence, occasionally cradling a cup of hot tea between his palms. None had been offered to me—to do so would have been impolite.

"You ask so little," he finally said.

"One man's trash, another man's treasure."

He bowed.

108

"Tax collectors may posture before frightened store owners, but they are nothing but servants themselves," I explained to Lamont. "They will have a specific route they are expected to cover. So they will come tonight. We cannot be certain of the time, but it will be after dark."

Lamont touched his knee with a length of rebar he had obtained—one end was wrapped in several layers of black tape. "Be easier to just pop them," he said. "Quicker, too. Too bad you threw away that pimp's piece, Ho."

"A bullet's path cannot be predicted. Nor can its consequences. I have seen men shot and continue on. I have seen bullets pass *through* men, and the bullets themselves continue on."

"You learned that in war, right?"

"Yes."

"I been to war, too, Ho. Let me tell you something about hitting a man in the head with a tire iron. Some, they get knocked out. Some, they don't hardly notice. And some, they get dead."

"We do not intend to—"

"Look, bro. You some kinda . . . yeah, I know, *not* a ninja, okay? But you got that . . . touch thing. Not me. I start whaling on some motherfucker with this, you never know how it's gonna turn out."

"I accept this," I said, watching surprise flit across Lamont's face. "There is yet another reason we could not use that weapon you took from the pimp. Bullets can be extracted, not only from a corpse, but from the living. Nor could we use it to threaten—you yourself said that this was not a weapon which would command respect on sight."

"So we want them to think it was . . . like, ghosts, right? Hit and run."

"That's the way it's *supposed* to be," Ranger said.

We both turned to look at him.

"See you at Brewster's," Ranger said. And then he was gone.

109

The two Chinese youths walked past Lamont and I as if we were crumpled pieces of paper on a dirty street. They were laughing between themselves when Lamont whipped his striking instrument at the knee of the one closest to us. Before that one had fallen, I was behind the other. It was over in seconds.

As Lamont and I moved off, the night air was ripped by a vampire's scream. Ranger descended upon the fallen youths, his matte black knife stabbing as methodically as a piston, over and over. Pedestrians began to scream. Ranger suddenly stopped, scanned the area, and fled in the opposite direction from the one Lamont and I had taken.

"Crazy motherfuc—"

"Not now," I said to Lamont.

As police sirens sounded, we turned the corner and made our way down behind the row of eating establishments. The delivery van was waiting, "Kabuki" emblazoned on its closed sides. The key was in the ignition.

As Lamont drove off, I prayed that Ranger's orgy of violence had not destroyed the sign I had placed so carefully on the bodies.

110

Behind Brewster's library, Michael was holding the bottom of a length of cargo netting. Lamont expertly maneuvered the van into place. Michael and Target each tied an end of the netting around the rear axle, then threw open the back doors.

Books began to flow.

Lamont, Target, and I loaded them into the van.

As the load increased, Target ran off. Michael took his place beside me. Lamont moved back behind the wheel.

A sharp *"Pssst!"* broke the silence. Michael did not hear it. But Michael had not been listening for it as I had. Perhaps some part of me even expected it.

Lamont's barely audible warning touched my center, transporting me back to when I first became a creature of dark nights spent in even darker alleys. My senses opened, guiding me to my left. I shifted position without moving, knowing that to alarm Michael could be fatal to our mission.

A police car stood at the mouth of the alley through which

we had entered. It was not moving. As I watched, the window closest to us slid down.

Data was being collected.

Data from which decisions would be made.

If the stream of books resumed with the police car still in place, the new data would become the decision.

Lamont had disabled the overhead light that turned on whenever the van's doors were opened, and greased the hinges and locks so heavily that they opened without a sound. His warning was also a message—Lamont had chosen to stand his ground.

Michael was too fragile to make such choices. I could not risk speaking, and if his own eyes detected the police car . . .

I put my hand on the back of Michael's neck, as if to get his attention. As he turned toward me, smiling, I used my thumb and forefinger to disconnect his brain from his body. I gently lowered him into a welcoming pool of shadow.

I then asked the night for permission to enter, knowing it might be my last such request. When it was granted, I moved toward the police car.

III

When an adversary has the ability to inflict harm from a distance, that distance itself is an adversary. A rifle that is capable of delivering death at one hundred meters is useless if the target can place himself between the tip of its barrel and the marksman holding it.

That is the essence of fear. Efforts to avoid it only magnify its power—fear is an enemy that can be killed only at close range.

Fear must always be acknowledged, but never respected. Only when such a state is achieved may fear become an invited visitor.

The closest range of all is intimacy. The deeper the fear is embedded in one's spirit, the more vulnerable it is.

As I closed the distance to the police car, I walled off everything outside the immediate task. If a single policeman were to walk down the alley, his flashlight would have far greater power than his pistol. He must be allowed to penetrate deeply enough into the darkness for me to disable him before the van was exposed, without alerting his partner. What was the range of his flashlight? Would his partner follow him into the dark . . . or would he use his radio to summon others?

If the police moved in, Lamont could vanish down the other end of the alley—but that would mean leaving the van in place. It could easily be traced, but the restaurant manager would quite truthfully deny any knowledge of its role in our book-transfer scheme. Without Lamont or Ranger present, the others were in no real danger. The books belonged to Brewster, and he was already "registered." Target would be judged as insane on the spot.

But the plan was our heartbeat.

With that sudden understanding came the answer to my strategic dilemma. I moved much closer than I had originally planned. Close enough to hear the policemen talking in a jargon I did not fully understand.

"A nose like that, fucking asshole should be working K-9, am I right? He'd make those dogs look like amateurs."

"Yeah. Only I got a better idea. How about if we put a leash on him and let him work the bomb squad?"

They both laughed, but there was an ugliness to their laughter that would not have comforted whoever they were talking about.

Just as I slithered out of the alley, a stream of expelled cigarette smoke from the opened window decoded their conversation. Apparently, another officer had complained about smoking in that particular car, and they had stopped so that they might enjoy their cigarettes in peace.

I moved to my left, walking in the opposite direction from the way the police car was facing. Once out of what I judged to be their visual range if they were using their mirrors, I crossed the street and worked my way toward them, until I was just across from the driver's open window.

I drew all doubt deep into my belly, held it for a moment, then released it through my nose, narrowing my focus. If the door closest to the alley opened and one of the policemen got out, I would have to cut the communications link between the police car and their headquarters *before* following the other officer down the alley from behind.

Having no choice but one brings great comfort.

The policeman behind the wheel snapped his cigarette into the street. It sparked briefly as it hit. The driver's window slid up as the police car pulled away.

112

Michael was still on the ground when I returned. I brought him back by reconnecting what I had temporarily blocked.

"What the . . . ?"

"You fainted," I whispered.

"I never—"

"It does not matter . . ." I began, just as what had earlier been a stream of books suddenly became a raging river. It was all the three of us could do to keep up, but either there were fewer books than Brewster had described or they took up less space than we had envisioned—only a few more minutes passed before the netting was empty.

Michael and I untied it, and watched as it was drawn back up into the building.

There was room in the back of the van for us all.

113

"Where's Ranger?" Gloria asked me, wiping sweat from her face. All the books had been transferred to the ACT basement, and we were about to return the van.

"He never appeared," I told her.

"Right" is all she said.

114

After that night, we never returned to the restaurant. Unlike the possibly mythical murder of a pimp who owned a white

Rolls-Royce, the newspaper had deemed the butchering of the two Chinese youths worthy of front-page coverage.

115

Weeks passed without a sign of Ranger. Michael, in particular, seemed to mourn his disappearance. As if in tribute to his friend's memory, he had entered some sort of "day program," and was learning computer-programming skills.

Brewster visited his library regularly, nearly always accompanied by Target.

Lamont filled his notebook, working every day, even while we were fishing.

116

I stood, a part of the darkness. I watched as Earl stepped out of the ACT building and took a position on the sidewalk, arms folded across his broad chest, as if standing guard over the empty building behind him.

Target suddenly appeared. As mysteriously as he had among us the first time. He approached Earl, who clearly had been expecting him. They went inside, together.

117

Michael, Brewster . . . and now Target.

As I fought to banish the encroaching smugness from my spirit, I sensed a presence behind me. I did not turn, accepting whatever was to come.

"I nailed the ear to the door of their joint." Ranger's voice. "It was easy to find—they got their name right over the door. Shadow Riders, Lamont said they were. I figured they'd know what it meant, the ear."

"What did it mean?" I asked, still not turning around.

"Some psycho Vietnam vet's on the loose," Ranger said, his clipped words as measured as a fire-walker's steps. "Probably can't tell one gook from another. Maniac like that's running around, you don't want to be going out for a stroll in the wrong neighborhood. Best stay close to home."

"Hai."

"That ear thing, I didn't plan it, Ho. It didn't come to me until the next morning, when I woke up behind a Dumpster. It was in my pocket. That's when I figured it out."

"But why were you even—?"

"Just backing you up, brother. That's what I told myself, anyway. Ranger, playing his role. I was on fixed post, across the street. That's why I swiped that pea-shooter from Lamont, just in case. When I saw you guys had it handled, I was going to fade. But when I saw them lying there, I just went . . ."

"Ah."

"Every night, I come by here."

I could think of nothing to say to that.

"I called Gloria," Ranger said. "She told me I have to come in. I know she's right. But I can't do it. I can't play that game anymore."

"Gloria is waiting for you, Ranger. She has not called the police. She has shown her trust."

"I know. But I'm not like that kid Brewster. That other

world of his, it's not such a bad place. It never . . . takes over, you know? He's still in touch. If you told him he could spend his whole life in that library of his if he wanted, he'd turn down the offer. Just like he wouldn't stay with his sister. He's some kind of crazy—that's the only way they take you where Gloria works—but he don't need to be locked up or anything."

"Brewster is not dangerous," I agreed.

"But if he had lost that damn library . . . who knows, right?"

"Hai."

"And now he won't. He's got a lot of worlds he lives in, but they're all home, see?"

"We all have a—"

"Remember when I told you that's what *we* used to call home, Ho. The World. Like, if we could just make it back here . . ."

"Ranger," I said, still with my back to him, "you did make it back. And you are here."

"But I'm not home, Ho. See, I'm not crazy. Maybe I was, once. But not for a long time now. Every time something . . . happens, the shrinks say, 'Ranger lost it,' like they're on my side. Like they understand. But they got it backwards. When they say I lost it, that's when I *found* it. Gloria, she's good people, but she doesn't get it. But you do, don't you, Ho? You always knew. I could tell."

"Brewster visits his sister—"

"When he *wants* to, Ho. Those people over there, they've got his back. They can . . . I don't know, help him deal. That's what they do, see? They don't try and fucking 'fix' you, like they do at the VA. They just give you . . . tools, like. And now you've even got Target hooked up, huh?"

"It was not I who—"

"Sure it was, Ho. You came to save us."

"No, no, Ranger. Please. I came to save myself."

"Sure, I got it," he said, as if placating a foolish child. "Where's Michael?"

"I do not—"

"Come on, Ho. This is me, Ranger. You think the door don't swing both ways? You know me. Inside me. The real me. It doesn't matter where Michael is, am I right?" he said.

"Yes," I said, wondering if Ranger's use of Michael's "closer" was unconscious mimicry . . . or showing me something I had failed to see before. Not in Michael; in Ranger.

"Michael, he went home. Just like you wanted. I saw Lamont before I came here. You know what he was doing?"

"Writing."

"He's home, too," Ranger said. "You came to save us all. Bring us home."

"Please," I begged the presence behind me. "I have no such—"

"Sure you do, bro. Like I said, I *know.* Where's *your* home, Ho?"

"I have no—"

"Yeah, you do. And you're already there."

I felt the shame of Ranger's truth. But before I could—I do not know the words—he spoke again:

"I go home, Ho. Then I come back. That's when I'm with you and the guys. Back to The World. That's not *my* home.

Every time I come back, I'm not coming home, I'm just . . . waiting."

"I, too, am—"

"No. Listen! I *like* doing it, Ho. Up close, with my knife. They probably got some special name for that, but I know what it really is. It's me. It wasn't me before—when I was psycho for real—but it is now."

"Ranger . . ."

"Don't even say it, Ho. It doesn't matter now. I wasn't born to be . . . whatever I am. And there's enough of my true self—remember how you're always saying?—there's enough of that left so I know what's right. It's slipping away from me, that part. I have to go before it's all gone."

"Can we not—?"

A soft *pop!* behind me was his answer. I spun around. Ranger was lying on the ground, that little pimp pistol in his hand, a small droplet of blood forming between his eyebrows.

I knelt, searching for what I knew I would not find. Ranger had returned to himself.

I bowed before the warrior who had chosen seppuku. Not for the selfishness of his own "honor," but to protect others from the beast within himself.

110

Winter has come.

We still have our dugouts, but most nights they are shared only by Lamont and myself. Target and Brewster still come and stay with us occasionally, but it is not the same.

Nor shall it ever be again. Brewster has a part-time job in

a used-book store. When he speaks of finding a place to live, he does not mean shelter for the night. Each passing day, he becomes less of our world.

Target has actually found a place to live—some sort of residential facility. He is not incarcerated, but free to come and go as he wishes. There are obviously some requirements attached to the food and housing provided him—whatever they might be, they do not frighten him. He continues to communicate in outbursts, but they are more muted, almost conversational.

At first, Lamont was pleased when either would appear. Now he is barely cordial. "They're not with us anymore, Ho. They found themselves a new crew."

"They found themselves," I said.

"Spare me, bro. That place they go, it's only for people who ain't right in the head. 'Specially that kid Brewster. He's always trying to sell me on the joint, like he's working on fucking commission. What would I want with a bunch of head doctors? I know how I got here. And it's where *I* want to be. *My* choice, okay?"

Michael never comes at all. Perhaps he found his white Rolls-Royce.

I cannot follow the man who finally freed me of those self-worshiping shackles I had forged and fastened around my own soul.

I had not truly known Ranger. But he had truly known me.

119

Finally, I know myself. Ranger said I had been sent to save our band. He believed this in his soul. His last act had been to remove my final burden, thus allowing the savior to complete his mission.

No wonder "mission" had always held such sacred meaning to my horribly wounded friend.

I found a proper resting place for Ranger's medal.

The warrior had gone to the only place where he might find peace.

120

Ranger's sacrifice was also his gift of truth.

I have learned that a man who counts himself a shepherd is not worthy to be a member of a flock.

This shall be my last night in the dugout. Tomorrow, I will bid farewell to my friend Lamont.

He has been anticipating this for some time, I know. Showing me how he had filled his notebook to the brim was his way of telling me he wanted to return to the field of battle and reclaim his heart.

121

Tomorrow, I begin again. I will walk, alone, until I come to where Chica waits.

May I be worthy when I kneel before her, and offer my final haiku.

The trampled flower
Blooms anew, beauty drawing
Father to daughter

ABOUT THE AUTHOR

Andrew Vachss has been a federal investigator in sexually transmitted diseases, a social-services caseworker, a labor organizer, and has directed a maximum-security prison for "aggressive-violent" youth. Now a lawyer in private practice, he represents children and youths exclusively. He is the author of numerous novels, including the eighteen-volume Burke series, two collections of short stories, and a wide variety of other material, including song lyrics, graphic novels, essays, and a "children's book for adults." His books have been translated into twenty languages, and his work has appeared in *Parade, Antaeus, Esquire, Playboy,* the *New York Times,* and many other forums. A native New Yorker, he now divides his time between the city of his birth and the Pacific Northwest.

The dedicated Web site for Vachss and his work is www.vachss.com.